Germano Romano

Crystal women.

Sara & Amina.

Two women, two personalities,
two temperaments.
Their lives met by chance,
tied up to the end.

To you, Giorgio.

Table of contents

The return.

I'm going home, my old happy years home. I hope that the train collects an impossible delay, so much so that it prevents me from arriving at my destination. I go back to where the memories await me greedily; lost in the alleys, forever hidden in the bowels. They are my only relatives, the only ones with which I would like to be in company. I decided to come by train because I prefer to be around people and not lock myself in the car alone.

As the train's brakes start to whistle, Sara has time to open her bag and quickly read, once again, that old yellowed folded sheet. She always carries it with her. She opens it for the thousandth time. It is a poem, which follows her everywhere, well-guarded; it is also part of her life.

"Cloud, cloud fleeing far away on the horizon,

You are woven with a thread of strength; your bonds are courage.

The wind that pushes you far away is not an enemy,

Nor is the sea that you look at from above an enemy.

I watch you from the shore as you........ "

She doesn't finish reading it, and puts it back in its place. Those verses no longer keep her company; they have become bitter. *We realize that we are like stones burned by the sun, when not even our dry tears wet our face.* At the same time, the conductor's announcement warns that they are about to enter the station and that passengers headed to Florence begin to prepare. She takes her luggage and stands in line waiting for the train to come to a complete stop. Finally, the doors open, she gets out with the bulky suitcase and a smaller one with a shoulder strap. As soon as she gets out of the train wagon, she sees the familiar platforms between the tracks; smells and strong emotions come back to her. After a deep breath, she heads for the taxis. Making the short journey from the station to the hotel, she leans out the window in an attempt to see as many details of the city as possible. The stone corners of its buildings, the tourists who crowd it in droves. She would like to avoid tourists, they do not know how to embrace this city, and they do not know how to love it as she loves it. The luminous air makes her feel a shudder all over her body, this is her city, the city where she lived better years and that she finally finds again. She is forty years old and she is beautiful, very white in complexion, perhaps too much. She was born and raised in England, but she inherited light brown hair and blue eyes from her Italian parents. Lying on the bed in the hotel room she would not want to go out, she would like to stay doing nothing, quiet until the following day, the big day when she would venture into her city after so many years. Instead, she immediately recovers from this torpor and, despite the February cold, she decides to wear a mini skirt with knee-high leather boots. She focuses on an exaggerated makeup: "OK, let's go now for a walk. Better if I go out for a while and maybe make friends with someone". She wanders a bit around her hotel; she wants to enjoy the sound of her heels on the cobblestone, the shops with elegant merchandise, the crisp air. So tired, she decides to go to a pub she knows and is curious to see again. She lifts her mini skirt a little, she wants to overdo it, and as soon as she arrives, she opens the door and enters without hesitation. Once inside, she feels a sense of embarrassment: the strong smell of the pub assails her immediately, that smell that instantly takes her back in time. She realizes almost immediately that it has become a bar for casual dating, but she does not give up, she intends not to follow any rules, she wants to drink to excite her mood more. That smell-filled air confuses her, and she can't decide where to sit. The bartender, attracted more by her sensuality than by her beauty, wastes no time and invites her to sit at the counter, "Hey, hello beautiful, you can sit at the counter if you want!" Then immediately after: "But you, you are ... you are ... yes, you are Sara! Welcome back, since when have you been in Florence?". "Incredible" Sara thinks, he remembers me! We only met a couple of times! The bartender adds, "I'm happy to see you. You are always the same... I mean ... You haven't changed at all, but sit here by the counter, let have a chat about the old days". In the meantime, he continues to look at her, without holding back, from the head, passing through the breasts well shown in the tight shirt, going down into the miniskirt, up to the shiny black boots, which make the bartender lose all control. He doesn't mind receiving any response from Sara, he just has to watch her settle down on a stool in front of the counter. Sara gives him a slight smile, and he: "My dear, are you here for a drink? I am happy to see you, today I offer to you what you want ... anything ... ". He doesn't imagine Sara despises him. She, showing an icy attitude, stretches out on the counter towards him, just to play with him for a while, uttering the words with sensual lips: "Hello handsome, yes, I'm back for a few days. Pass me a dark beer". The bartender hands it to her, smiling and staring at her. After having taken the beer, she gets up from the stool and looks for a free seat; indeed, she takes the opportunity to observe the place and realizes that everything has changed. She glimpses of an empty seat at a table and, as she reaches it, the bartender insists: "How long has it been since we last met? Let me think ... long time. Maybe seven or eight years? Besides, that friend of yours? That little girl who worked here?" Sara doesn't want to waste time with him, she doesn't even answer; she looks around and asks her table neighbor if he has a cigarette. The boy offers it to her immediately, he was waiting for nothing else, and with a southern accent, while he hands her the cigarette: "Hello beautiful, all alone?", And Sara: "Maybe ...". The boy insists: "I would say yes, apparently. Come; take a seat at my table". Sara, in order to harm the bartender, immediately accepts the invitation by moving to his table with the beer. The bartender, however, does not give up, observes everything with growing

8

disappointment. "So where are you from, beautiful?" and Sara, "From hell". The boy, taking off his jacket, and showing his arms with extended and colorful tattoos, insists, "I like hell, it's hot, sensual and then there are so many sins to do there", then he gets too close to Sara. The bartender is increasingly furious, perched on the counter, as a vulture does not miss a word of the conversation, until he decides to join too "So Sara, that girl, that friend of yours, how is she?" The bartender's question irritates Sara; she suddenly becomes serious and stands up. She leaves the beer on the table, gets up to leave, when the boy at the table with a quick move blocks her by holding her wrist: "Hey, where are you going, stay here with me having fun", the bartender is ready to intervene, but Sara sneaks off easily, doesn't answer and heads for the exit. The boy remains silent, perhaps surprised, while the bartender yells behind her to re-credit his hopes: "Bye Sara, see you soon, come back whenever you want". Sara leaves without even looking back or saying goodbye. As soon as she leaves, she regrets the pantomime she staged in the smelly pub. She goes to bed and ends the day, but as always, she takes the little poem out of her bag, reads again it for a few lines and then falls asleep sweetly. The next morning, she gets up early, she hasn't slept much. She gets ready wearing pants with a thigh-length jacket and a padded cape to protect herself from the February cold. As soon as she leaves the hotel, she goes to the first destination of her tour. She would like to have breakfast, but she is in a hurry. While she is in the street, she begins to feel confused, her head sways a little, she stops, leans against the wall of a long building with the plaster a little chipped. The city is invaded by carnival, colorful confetti; people with carnival dress that enjoy screaming aloud and filling the air with noises. She has just crossed piazza di "Santa Maria del Fiore", but she does not go along de Martelli Street, she prefers the narrowest street of the Saint Lorenzo district. As she walks down the street, she feels a sense of suffocation; she yearns for the large space of the square, her final goal. She hurries, but cannot breathe, when she reaches the end of the Saint Lorenzo Street, she turns left, keeping her eyes closed. When she opens them, the silent facade of the church of Saint Lorenzo stands out in front of her. She is fascinated: "Well, thank goodness it wasn't completed; it would have been too much for such a perfect monumental church." Party people disturb her, just as colors thrown into the air invade the beauty she wishes to savor. She is about to faint, she stops for a moment, unable to keep standing: "The suspense of the hidden treasures behind the silent facade is too strong". She graduated in literature, specialized in the restoration of monuments; she knows the church of Saint Lorenzo well. She visited it several times when she lived in Florence, but this time it is different, this time she is more fragile. She heads towards the entrance, trying to ignore the tourists that are intent on celebrating and photographing, unaware of the value of the square that hosts them. Looking at them with pride: "This city should be closed to those who are not sensitive to these monuments. This city is not for everyone". She remains motionless for a moment before entering, she feels like she no longer feels her body, and she feels like she has turned into a cloud. Then nothing.

She recovers finding herself on the ground with those same tourists, previously snubbed, who now help her. They explain to her in various languages that an ambulance is coming, but Sara sits up and assures them all that she is okay. The ambulance arrives and the first checks begin; they ask her something, but she thanks them, she just has a strong desire to get out of that crowd. The doctor insistently invites her to go to the hospital for further tests as he has detected an excessive tachycardia. Sara, to get rid of him, replies that she feels like she has had a tachycardia, followed by difficulty in breathing and consequent dizziness, after which she fainted out. She adds angrily "What do you want now? I fainted out; can't it happen? Leave me alone", these last words are almost screamed. The doctor, while realizing that the patient is coming out of a mental confusion, gives in to the woman's rude insistence and decides to leave. However, before to leave, he asks her to fill out forms and sign it. Sara signs without wasting any more time and gets out of the ambulance. Then she is alone, so she hurries to enter the church.

As soon as she is inside, the melodious architecture of a very different world from the outside, welcomes her. She is calm again, serene, in the center of the main nave, what she identifies as an ancient street lined with round arches. The facades of this street are tremendously slender in height because of the capitals and the overhanging pulvinus. "My good Brunelleschi, here too you have brought in the external space. You have delimited this street with the same architecture as the "Ospedale degli Innocenti" ("Hospital of the Innocent" children hospital). The proportion of the church central aisle is perfect, and Sara's incorporeal nature pushed by the thrill of so much perfection expands to the sides of the central aisle, meets the side chapels, where, following the perfect proportions, it further widens. Until she stops abruptly, the shallow depth of the side chapels blocks her. She upset yells: "Why? Why you, Brunelleschi, did not bring the proportion even in the chapels! ". Someone turns to her, thinking that she is addressing those present. Sara ignores them and, from the limited space of the side chapels, directs her gaze upwards. She would like to fly elate with harmony, up to the elegant proportion of the high round arch vault, which is the natural end of the nave. Nevertheless, boom, her disembodied nature hits the coffered ceiling: "No, it's too much, I have to escape from here, and I have to take refuge in one of the two lateral lungs ". She goes towards the new sacristy, then thinks about it: "I know very well that it is another world, it is a perfect architecture with an excess of decorative language". She swerves to the old sacristy, where she arrives out of breath. She only manages to calm down as soon as she finds the perfect harmony of the cubic space. She relaxes and turns her gaze towards the hemispherical umbrella-shaped dome, which, for her perfection, makes her smell art with her eyes closed. When she reopens them, Donatello's decorations disturb her, and again, aloud: "Why? Why, you Donatello try to obscure this harmonious architecture? ".

Outside, the carnival is raging. It is time for lunch, and the monumental church empties, indeed perhaps only she remains, satisfied by this loneliness. While she is still confused, immersed in these sensations, she sees a group of people in carnival dresses of a bygone era. This group almost rushes into the old sacristy. They intrigue Sara, she notices that those people are not happy, they are nervous; they were arguing with each other. Only now, she sees among them a woman who, walking fast drags with her a little girl of about five or six years. The woman turns to see if the pursuers are reaching her. When she realizes she is being reached, she curses the four men who are about to block her. Sara has a shiver of fear; she tries to hide. The woman quickens her steps, still holding the little girl tightly, but the four men decide to end it, they take out some knives and grab the woman, yank her while one of them tries to separate her from the little girl. The fight is violent, Sara observes the scene petrified, cannot move a muscle. Three men hold the woman still, while the fourth snatches the girl from her arms and drags her away, the other three in the meantime stab the woman irritated by her sharp screams of terror. The woman falls lifeless to the ground in a puddle of blood. Then the three killers reach the fourth man, who in the meantime lets the girl slip out of hand. One of the three men, as soon as he notices it, throws a knife at the girl to stop her, hitting her in the back, so that the little girl falls to the ground. They reach her and pick her up, then run away. As the little girl tried to escape in terror, she caught Sara's attention, holding out her small hand, hoping for her help. Only now Sara manages to let out a scream of terror, she is shocked. This scream draws the attention of the four killers to her. These are moments of terror. The men look at each other without knowing what to do. Then, after a last knowing glance, two of them head towards Sara, brandishing the knives still stained with blood. Sara can't escape, her legs are nailed. She sees the two approaching quickly, getting closer and closer with knives in hand, only now she screams as she manages to turn around in an attempt to escape, but she feels a strong hit to the head. Then, the absolute emptiness.

In a white room, illuminated by a diffused light, Sara barely opens her eyes, but the light forces her to close them immediately. She feels relaxed, almost drugged. When she finally manages to open her eyes fully, she thinks for a moment that she is in her hotel room. Soon after realizes she is somewhere else, in a white, light-flooded room. She sees machinery on the wall and a drip in her arm connected to a hanging hook. She tries to get up, but she can't and asks for help. Nobody comes, she still tries to get up, but her head is still spinning, she can barely sit on the bed. Finally, a nurse enters her room, but Sara screams, believing to be still in danger. The nurse tries to calm her down, tells her to relax and not to worry, that she is in a hospital room. Sara calms down, realizes she is saved from the attack; somehow, she managed to escape those killers. However, at the memory of what happened to her, she falls back in terror. Meanwhile, the nurse has already called for help, a second nurse rush into the room and the two decide to administer a sedative as prescribed by the doctor. Sara would like to say something, but her tongue is stuck, weak and, despite her, she returns to a deep sleep. It is early in the morning when someone wakes her up, the doctor, busy in the morning visits, keeps her pulse and decides to stop all treatments. The patient is now alert and calm. He calls her by name: "Sara, Sara don't worry I'm the doctor, I'm here to help you, you're in the hospital. How do you feel now? Yesterday you were very agitated, we gave you a sedative". Sara is serene, this long rest has invigorated her, she looks around and asks the doctor if she is now safe, and if they have captured those killers? The doctor is surprised: "Sara, don't worry, everything is fine, you are in a hospital room, rest and don't think about anything. We carry out other analyzes and decide how to continue". Sara realizes that the doctor does not know anything about she has been assaulted, thus she begins to get nervous again "I was agitated! Sure, I was someone was killing me. I don't even know how I escaped. They had caught up with me and had bloody knives. They killed that woman and maybe the little girl too. Doctor, do you understand I'm in danger? Please help me, let me speak to the police. Which hospital am I in?" Sara tries to get up, but this time she feels a pain in her head and realizes that it is being bandaged. She realizes to be injured and allows the nurses to lay her on the bed, until the doctor, a little annoyed, "Sara you need to rest, when you fell you hit your head violently. Clinical tests are underway to identify any bleeding, and until then it would be better if you stay relaxed without making any effort. You must remain calm and serene. We have no contact with your family; if you want us to call any of them you should give us at least some telephone numbers". Sara gets more and more agitated, "Doctor, how can I be calm and serene! Someone tried to kill me, you have to protect me, I want the police. No, I have no family, yes friends, but for the moment, I don't want to disturb them. I will get in touch with them as soon as possible. Where is my cell phone?" She begins to fidget again, showing that she does not trust the doctor and the nurses, so much so that the doctor is forced to inject her again with a light dose of sedative. The doctor gives instructions to supervise her until they can reach a family member and not before the result of the CT scan. The next day everything is calm. Sara is still lying on the bed in silence. A nurse notices that she is about to wake up and, according to the instructions, immediately calls the doctor. In the meantime, Sara seems to be calmer as soon as she wakes up, she got over the shock she had fallen into the day before. As soon as the doctor enters the room, he is pleased to see that the patient has overcome the trauma. He rejoices and tells her that her CT scan shows nothing, no wound, there is no bleeding, apart from a small injury to the skull which, however, has no effect other than occasional headaches for a few days. Sara feels that in order to leave, she has to prove that she is serene. She fears that they will keep her in that room against her will for who knows how long. She thanks them, showing herself docile, and, settling on her bed, calmly explains what happened to her during her visit to the church of Saint Lorenzo. This time the doctor begins to believe her, and he suspects that something has really happened to her, so asks a nurse to bring the patient's personal effects, those found next to her when she was unconscious in the church's Old Chapel. Before calling the police, the doctor wants to check whether there has been a theft, and therefore an assault for the purpose of theft. The tourists who found her unconscious lying on the ground, and who alerted the police, did not speak of aggression. The police officers, who rushed to the scene, having just inspected everything, believed that the woman had probably tripped and hit her head on the edge of the base of the pillar. Indeed, they found no signs of a struggle or any clue that might suggest violence. Sara determinedly continues to insist that she was attacked, that there were four men in carnival dresses, chasing a woman. As she explains what happened, the nurse arrives with her personal belongings, so Sara goes through her purse and verifies that nothing is missing. The doctor is once again skeptical of the woman's story and asks her if she really wants the police to intervene! Sara resolutely insists. In the meantime, there is no longer any reason to keep her in the hospital, they also remove the bandage from her head and decide to discharge her. They escort her to the hotel, where the police had already notified every one of the incident. They had taken care to vacate her room so she wouldn't pay for the empty days, as they didn't know how long she'd been in the hospital. They stored her luggage at the back of the reception, but as soon as they saw her return, happy to see her recovered, they immediately put her in another room. In the afternoon, a police inspector arrives at the hotel accompanied by a police officer to collect the testimony. Sara repeats for the umpteenth time the action she witnessed, and the aggression suffered. The inspector questions her repeatedly, making her repeat her story continuously. Sara undaunted always repeats it without ever contradicting herself or changing anything, however the story is very strange and not very trustworthy. There are no witnesses and no traces of blood from the woman with the child. Sara swears the floor was covered with blood from the stab wounds; she makes a very realistic description of it. The commissioner does not respond immediately to this strange story but assures Sara that he will carry out further and more accurate investigations. In the meantime, he makes sure she doesn't need anything and asks for the address of some family member or friend of hers. Sara is still afraid of those men; she assumes and suspects that they can go back to finish their work. The inspector advises her to keep calm and rest, then asks her again for the contacts of relatives or friends of hers. Sara repeats that she has no family and that she is alone, but she does not even decide to give him an address of her friends; she will notify them as soon as possible, as she assures the investigators. The commissioner has nothing to do but leave, but before he suggests her not to leave the hotel, he would call her back, at the latest tomorrow, in the late morning for any developments. Left alone, Sara locks herself in the room, doesn't dare to go out. She is tempted to call her Florentine friends, but then she thinks back, she has caused them so many worries in recent times, and she doesn't want them to pity her by always showing up with other problems. She prefers to call them only when the investigations clarify what happened. They know that she is in Florence, but they also know that she wants to be alone for a few days. She tries to relax, turns on the television and asks for a strong cocktail at the hotel bar. She dines in her room and even manages to sleep. The next day, in the late morning, the inspector summons her to his office, and Sara rushes there thinking there is some news. This time she finds the inspector impatient and nervous. The inspector shows her the doctor's report, the one they had drawn up when Sara fainted in front of the church of Saint Lorenzo. He explains: "Madam, the doctor's report recorded symptoms such as: tachycardia, dizziness, fainting, mental confusion, as well as difficulty breathing. To these symptoms", he stops for a moment and looks at Sara with disapproval, "to these symptoms there are also others such as hallucinations and a sense of terror, exactly those you had in the old sacristy of the church. I talked to the doctor about the report, and he explained that you had Stendhal syndrome. I'm sorry, but I think the doctor is right if we also take into consideration the subsequent events: the people in costume, the aggression ..." Sara interrupts him stating firmly that she is not crazy, that she was attacked and that she really saw everything she said. That she also received a hit to the head, perhaps to stop and suppress her as being the only witness. While Sara desperately tries to make herself believed, the inspector has a lot more to do than waste time with a tourist with Stendhal syndrome and insists that there is no evidence of this assault, that Sara would be the only witness and that no one, in such a crowded place, has seen anything. Furthermore, there is no trace of blood, nor has there been any reported murder, kidnapping, or disappearance of anyone in the last few days. Sara would like to answer, but the inspector interrupts the conversation and advises her to go back to the hospital and not to the police station. Before letting her go, he has some compassion and decides to give his business card to her, begging her to use it in case of real need. He hopes Sara can feel more protected and comfortable with this small sign of understanding. Sara leaves nervous and disheartened, no one believes her. Once in the hotel, she is alone, alone with the terror she felt a few days before. She refuses to believe she had a fit of insanity, or as they called it, Stendhal Syndrome. She is locked in her room, does not want to go out, she is tenaciously persuaded that those people were real and that sooner or later they can return to finish the job left unfinished. The attack took place at a time when the tourists were at lunch, but on the other hand, there are no signs of aggression, no bloodstains! Moreover, could someone has wiped the blood to hide the attack? "Yes, it's true, maybe someone cleaned the blood, maybe the sacristan? Now I call the commissioner to inform him of this eventuality". Then she thinks about it: they wouldn't believe it, and then to accuse a parish priest or someone from the church, that's nonsense. She would like to call her two friends: Cristian and Cris, but she prefers to wait anyway, she has to get by on her own. She has already involved her friends too much in the past in dangerous stories, and then, they had advised her against returning to Florence alone. Stubbornly that same afternoon, she decides to return to the church of Saint Lorenzo. She needs a lot of courage to go back to where she was attacked. Maybe the killers are still waiting for her there! She sets off with determination, gathering courage, at least until she catches a glimpse of the silent facade of Saint Lorenzo from a distance on the other side of the square. Soon she is overwhelmed by the panic of the memory of the attack. Approaching the monument, she begins to feel tachycardia, dizziness, but she gets stronger, she doesn't want to faint anymore and do another show. As soon as she walks in, she sits on a bench out of breath; she begins to cry from nervous tension, hiding her face in her hands. A guardian notices the scene and approaches her gracefully and asks her if she needs help! Sara thanks him, replies that she is fine. Then she decides to ask him for help, "Excuse me, can I ask you if it is possible to meet the priest in charge? Could I see him briefly for an urgent question? Please". The guardian explains to her that there is no parish priest today, and that in any case it is not so easy to meet him because he always has many appointments. She also needs to book an appointment. Sara stages a heavy cry, until the man, in order not to disturb the tourists, begs her to follow him into the sacristy; there they probably should at least find the vicar. Sara follows the man until they reach a small room, but not the sacristy she expected. A tall, thin young man is intent on talking to an elderly woman, and they both turn to Sara as soon as she enters, preceded by the guardian. The man approaches the vicar and whispers something in his ear, whispers and whispers again ... In the end, the vicar makes Sara sit in and with this excuse liquidates the old woman, who obviously was a boring guest. Sara immediately begins to tell him her story, and the parish priest listens patiently. He is surprised; he marvels and begins to doubt that the woman is very sane. Despite everything, he, pushed by Sara, decides to accompany her to the place of the alleged crime. Arriving at the old sacristy, Sara is a little afraid to enter, but then she strengthens herself and, holding on to the prelate's arm, she enters decisively. She looks closely at the floor and everything but finds nothing strange. She examines and investigates a little bit everywhere, but she finds nothing at all. She asks if they've scrubbed the floor and the answer is: no from last three days. Sara is stunned and asks her interlocutor if he has seen something strange, news of any attacks and if he has questioned the employees? The guardian is there with them, and rushes to make sure that he too has not seen anything, and nothing has happened in this sacristy, nor in the church. The prelate confided to Sara that the police came a couple of times to investigate but did not explain what exactly they were looking for or what had happened in the church. He learned that a woman fell; maybe she tripped and hit her head, so she was transported to the hospital. Only now the guardian recognizes Sara, he was the first to rush with the tourists, and he himself still assures that there were no signs of aggression. The prelate adds that the police had not told him what Sara just explained, so now he is surprised and shocked. Now Sara fears that they think she is crazy, that the two men may call the police by not trusting this strange woman. She sadly greets the parish priest and leaves quickly, before the man decides to call the police. Yet she is still not convinced.

Returning to the hotel, her attention is captured by a man sitting at a table of the restaurant-bar, on the sidewalk in front of her hotel. She realizes it because the man, no longer young, but handsome, looks at her insistently; "Maybe he's a harasser!" she thinks, and she goes straight to the hotel. As soon as she arrives at the reception of her hotel, they tell her that a man has asked for her, but he hasn't added anything, not even his

name. Sara is surprised, she asks for details, and
when the door attendant describes a person
similar to the one she just saw outside sitting at
the table, she rushes out instantly, but there is no
one at that table anymore. She doesn't
understand, maybe it's just a coincidence! On the
other hand, are the killers really haunting her?
She is confused and scared more than the last
few days. She returns to her room, but from time
to time, peeking through the shutters, she scans
passersby. She fears that it is her turn now, that it
is her turn to die, and that the man is a hitman!
However, she is now forced to put these fears
aside; she freshens up and leaves immediately.
Before leaving the hotel, she looks around to
make sure there are no suspicious people, then,
in a hurry, she walks towards the monumental
cemetery. She reaches the family tomb, where
her parents also wanted to be buried. Her parents
moved to Britain before she was even born.
Unfortunately, they died soon, when she was still
sixteen, being an only child, she had to continue
her life alone. Yet, despite these adversities, she
managed to embark on a commendable
university career, the same one that, at the
beginning of her career, took her to Palermo for a
one-year PhD. She sits silently in front of the
tombstone, a very high white marble tombstone
with some niches closed by marble hatches. Sara
does not dwell on that of her parents, but with her
hand, she delicately touches one of the two
names written on the tombstone below, names
written in brass letters. She remains so for a long
time, absorbed, moving away only with the

thought. Images and sections from her past, flow before her eyes, as fast as a film projected at high speed. She remains absorbed until she realizes that it is now evening. She walks away from the tombstone and, without looking back, heads for the exit. She returns on foot, as she came, she wants to walk and relax by observing the shop windows and the people on the street. She finally reaches the restaurant that overlooks her hotel. She enters without even paying attention to those present, looks around a bit and finds an empty table. The waiter asks her if she wants to have dinner, "Sure", she replies in a somewhat abrupt manner. She sits down at the table and relaxes while consulting the menu. The waiter waits next to her, Sara signals him to wait a moment, and then gives him the order. Only now, waiting for the order, as soon as she looks around, she flinches, she freezes. Not far, sits the man she had seen a few hours before at the tables outside the restaurant. Probably the same one that had come to ask for her at the reception. She is disoriented, but not frightened; indeed, she is in a crowded restaurant and does not believe it is possible to be attacked in front of all these witnesses! The man realizes that Sara has noticed him, and he doesn't get upset, he continues to look at her as if he wanted to entice her to a reaction. Sara is again assailed by terror; she has been so stressed recently that she no longer has the strength to react. Without thinking, she decides to get up and run away, she doesn't even wait for the waiter with her order. She rushes out, crosses the street and enters her hotel then locks herself in the room. She is sure that it is now her turn to die. From behind the curtains, she tries to see if that man comes out to follow her. She would like to call the police, now she has proof that someone is following her, perhaps to kill her. She stands still and watches for about an hour whoever goes out or enters the bar. In the meantime, she changes her mind and doesn't call the police, she fears she won't be believed yet. She wonders if it was just a coincidence, if that man only wanted to know her because he was attracted to her! An Italian molester ... she finally undresses and lies down on the bed hoping to sleep.

Memories.

She spends the night unable to sleep; she is obsessed with many memories. She lies down on the bed in the half-dark room, lit only by the streetlight, while the memories of the past come back to her. "When I was a university researcher in Palermo ..." Sara meditates ... she remembers the intense sunlight of that city. "About thirteen years ago, maybe twelve! I went to that beautiful southern capital for a PhD: Palermo". She totally indulges in her memories.

We are in Palermo, thirteen years earlier.

Work, just work. I am tired of only studying and working. That pub near my apartment, looks nice, with nice people, I never go there. How stupid I am, but that's enough, after work I go there. Sara doesn't even care how she is dressed, she doesn't care about these formalities, she has her head immersed in studies and university projects. Arrived at the appointed time: Finally, here I am in the pub, I don't want to seem disoriented. Well, now I sit down at one of the outdoor tables and try to stretch out. I read the menu to decide what to take, I hear a woman's voice addressing me, "Good afternoon, do you already prefer to order or I am waiting for you to call me?" Without looking up, I reply that I would have called her, as soon as I am ready. The waitress has just turned to leave when, looking up, I see her for the first time. She has short curly raven-colored hair, amber skin with a light shade. She is thin and not very tall. She intrigues me so I decide to call her back immediately. She turns, looks at me in amazement, while I remain silent. She has a light in her big black eyes, a doe look. She asks me "Please what do you prefer to order... please Miss.... Have you decided what to order?" Finally, she shuts up too we both remain silent. A few seconds pass during which, spontaneously and suddenly, a storm of electricity had broken out between us. Then the waitress, recovering from her unexpected silence, renews the request to be able to write the order. I too recover immediately and ask for a cocktail. She writes my order in her booklet and turning to enter the room, she sends me one last indecipherable glance. After a while, she arrives with my very flashy cocktail in the middle of a tray not up to the height of the cocktail. This time she no longer looks me in the eye as she did before, now she looks embarrassed and avoids my gaze. Well, then it's done, and yet I still have a doubt. She is certainly a foreigner, perhaps on the other side of the Mediterranean, and perhaps I misunderstood her approach to me, she is probably just shy, not used to certain things. Nevertheless, yes, what could the girls on the other side of the Mediterranean do! I don't give up easily, so I stubbornly decide to continue exploring; I was attracted to her. I stay at the table just long enough to finish my cocktail, and then ask for the bill. A guy brings it, and as I leave the money with a tip, I try to peer beyond the waiter to see if the doe is intentionally hiding in the room or is really busy with other customers. I come home accompanied by a sense of bitterness for not being able to go further. The next day, when I get home from work, I go straight to the same bar. She comes again, she doesn't smile at me, on the contrary she is still embarrassed, evidently, she is ashamed of something! Something she didn't do but would like to do? I realize that I am traveling in a sea that perhaps exists only in my imagination. However, I want to insist, I give her big smiles and I try to show myself as much as possible. I am sitting with my back straight and chest out, just to show more of my already plentiful breasts. Another day passes. Even today, I intend to go back to that bar. For the occasion, I wore a dizzying miniskirt, so much so that at work they were amazed: they always saw me in trousers. Unfortunately, this time too there are only a few sneaky glances between us; hardly any conversations, despite the fact that I tried to get her to talk. Well, she will be too busy with the many customers! I come home accompanied again by bitterness and even disappointment. What a fool I am, unable to make friends! We continued with these furtive glances for a few more days, until one evening I ask her, "What's your name?" She, surprised, without looking at me, in a low voice: "Amina". Then she stands staring at the ground as if, revealing her name, she had undressed. "Mine is Sara", even though she didn't ask me.

The next few days are more fruitful, we start having short conversations. The doe seems to have melted; she confided to me that she comes from the other side of the Mediterranean, and that she works illegally because she came clandestine on a refugee's boat with her two brothers. She too had to look for a job, against the wishes of her family, only because they desperately need the money. I also knew her age: seventeen. She is small; she is ten years younger than I am. I noticed that she always wears fairly baggy pants in the same color as the uniform of the waitresses in the bar, but unlike her, the other waitresses wear a mini skirt. She evidently has special permission not to have to wear the skimpy garment! However, the shirt, low-cut and tight like the other waitresses, highlights her small breasts and slim waist. I can guess, under those baggy pants, some round but really round hips. Her fleshy mouth, accomplice of those black eyes, confuses me and excites me more and more. Finally, one evening I convinced her to take a ride together after work. Maybe she accepted with a little reluctance, only then I realized that it is difficult for her to break free as her siblings constantly check on her. To overcome her indecision, I suggest her to leave work a couple of hours early, without saying anything at her house. To my amazement and joy, the girl accepts without thinking twice. She is beautiful and young, like me. Finally, the next day, two hours before the end of her shift, I go to pick her up. Amina imagines that we will go for a walk, so she thinks. I wasted too much time convincing her to meet me, now it's time to know if we really understood each other! I want her; I want this toy. To avoid excuses or resistances from the beginning, I tell her that we should go to my house for just a

30

moment because I fear I have left the oven on with a cake being cooked. A clear and banal excuse, but she believes it, she is totally naive and inexperienced, which is comforting to me as it is certainly easier for me to take her where I want. We go into my house, the hovel I have rented. As soon as she enters, she realizes that maybe she made a mistake! Yet she trusts me, a woman like her. I tell her to sit on the sofa; in the meantime, I stage the pantomime of running into the kitchen to check if the oven was really still on. "Thank goodness, luckily, I had turned it off. Come on, now that we're here, I'll make you a cocktail like the ones you know how to do well at the bar", and without waiting for her response, fearing rejection, I immediately prepare a cocktail for her and me. When I arrive with the two full glasses, I sit defiantly right next to her, our thighs almost touching. Again, the stupid girl lowers her gaze, but I make her look up handing her cocktail, I don't know if she wants it or not, but she doesn't have the courage to refuse. We drink and talk for a while; we look at each other with eyes that, in truth, speak together with our mouths. I don't have the courage to make the first move, so I decide to make another cocktail, and then another until the magical moment arrives when we get tired of talking and are ready for action. I place my hand on her leg, and then I squeeze it lightly, almost a gesture of friendship, a little out of the ordinary. I fear that my gesture may make her flee, but I realize that she has a thrill of pleasure. That's enough for me, I take her, hug her and kiss her. She does not react, rigid as a statue, does not move. I break my ardor for a second, only to ask her if she likes to be kissed! She does not answer me but neither does she refuse. Despite everything, I decide to give her some time, so I get up and go to the bathroom with an excuse, only to allow her to run away in the meantime, if she wants. After a few minutes, when I go back to the room, I find her still there, sitting, but this time she shows all her doe gaze. I approach, I sit next to her and kiss her again, an interminable kiss, during which I begin to touch her all over. She continues to remain rigid; obviously, she doesn't know what to do. I decide to undress her, forcing her hesitation to go on, I begin to touch her, to push her to feel pleasure, more and more. I haven't undressed yet, I prefer to continue like this, wanting to give her immediate pleasure and totally involving the outside of her sex. After a while the little girl gives up and lets out little moans, just enough to make me understand that she is consenting. Her small breasts are turgid; I can finally make her estranged from reality, completely. She is now abandoned in my arms and in my mouth; I thought she was different; I didn't think I could make her enjoy like this from the first date. I undress too and push her to do to me what I do to her. She can't satisfy me, at least for this first time. I'm sure I gave her a pleasure she had never experienced before. She later confessed to me that before she did not know her body. The evening comes fast and unwanted. We remain so entwined for some hours; this experience was wonderful for her, almost a discovery. On the other hand, I am a bit tired;

indeed, I am surprised to be refractory, probably because she remains clinging to me without detaching herself! The thing is, I want to be alone, so I kindly point out that it's late at night. Amina as she was awakened from a dream, she jumps up, she dresses faster than lightning without ever saying a word. However, before running out, she gives me a passionate kiss, the first on her own initiative.

The following days we always meet at my house, regularly. She explained to her brothers that she has extended her daily working hours, I don't know how will she justify that she doesn't have a pay raise for these extra hours? She becomes more and more self-confident, and I can always do what I want to her, without finding any resistance. From the external sexual pleasure, a little at a time, I was able to make her feel a more intense pleasure: I am an expert. Day after day, without realizing it, we bond more and more to each other, and I have no longer felt refractory towards her, at least almost never. A special bond has been created between us, as if we were one flesh. Usually I decide, she prefers to follow me like a naive sheep, but very confident in me. One Sunday morning in late spring, she unexpectedly manages to come to me all day, freeing herself from her brothers. After having had sex for hours, and our cravings satisfied, almost suddenly, we decide, or rather I decide, it's time to penetrate her for the first time. I am an expert, and she has never resisted my desires. I start with the usual kindness, but then, I don't know why, I continue with a little bit of violence. I don't want her to

simply have fun, I want to make her suffer a little. She goes through everything without rebelling; she feels pleasure only by blindly relying on me. For her it's always the "first time" for everything. She is completely in love with me; but I? Maybe, indeed, I certainly love her, but I'm afraid of a relationship with a person who totally depends on my lips. We have become inseparable, so much so that I will also have to introduce myself to the brothers to gain their trust and to be able to get Amina out of the house even if for a walk. One evening at the bar, while she brings me my usual order, now just an excuse to meet us, she places it on the table, and without saying a word goes back to the kitchen. I am amazed, it is very strange, and maybe I was wrong in something! May she be rethinking us! I remain at the table without being able to make a decision, whether to chase her into the kitchen or wait for her to come out and come back to me. I drink my tea and, when I take the napkin, I notice that there is a folded sheet inside. I don't know why but I immediately think of a "goodbye" in writing or some such nonsense; I begin to get angry. I open it, it's a poem:
"I whispered it to the birds of the sky.

I whispered it to the trees of the forest,

To fish in the sea.

I whispered it to you too my love".

I am moved as I read it, now I understand that we are united forever. Even if then, jokingly, I ask her not to understand what she had whispered to me and to all the others?

Four happy months pass, during which we meet regularly but always with subterfuge to divert the control of her two brothers. Then, finally, an idea comes to me: I would have offered Amina a job, yes, as my collaborator, necessary for the university research work I do in Palermo. I just have applied for a secretary, and I earn enough to pay her the same paltry salary that she earns at the bar. Amina's new position will justify our acquaintance with her siblings. Amina goes further, she confesses that she can no longer be without me even for an hour a day, but I am a bit hesitant. I explain to her that I too would like to live with her. We have already organized to get her fired from the bar and help me as a secretary in my research work... but to live together.... I don't know ... I don't know if I'm capable of it. This project stays locked in a drawer for some time, until one day Amina tells me that one of her brothers now has a secure job, so he brings his wife and four children home. The other brother intends to go to France; he looks like he has a chance for a better job. So only Amina remains in her brother's house in Palermo. I realize that she has a little fear and many doubts about her future life as a sister-in-law, as a perhaps unwelcome guest, certainly with a role of house cleaner or servant in her brother's house. Well, I finally make up my mind, take her out of that family and take her with me. The next day I get ready, I dress formally and when the bar closes, I go to get Amina. I hadn't warned her that I wanted to carry out our cohabitation project immediately, I want to surprise her. "Hello Amina", "Hello dear" she replies with her smile that makes her beautiful, even more beautiful, and that fills her face. I take her by the hand on the sidelines, out of the indiscreet eyes and ears, and I declare to her, in a formal way, almost like an official declaration of marriage, "I want you to come and live with me, I cannot kneel, but it is as if I did". She has no words. She can only make a look of wonder; her eyes sparkle with emotion. This is all we can do; we can't declare our love from the rooftops, I can't kneel and give her the engagement ring in a theatrical way in front of everyone. Apart from the fact that I don't put my feelings in public, but mostly because we are not allowed to do that. Amina lights up, throws her apron in the air and runs to get her things. She greets everyone in the bar, and we go out together. We would like to hug each other, but we cannot in front of everyone, even this is forbidden to us. However, who cares I think, and I try to hug her, but she is wiser, she blocks me and reminds me of social conventions; we have to hide and we always hide. Holding each other embraced, as two women are allowed to do (certainly never two men); we quickly walk towards her brother's house. We arrive at the building, Amina nervously opens the door, shaking with her hand, and then we quickly run over to the fourth floor. Before opening the door, we take a breath; we look at each other and yes, we are determined to do so. Right inside the first person I see is the sister-in-law, a dull woman, with a limp body despite her young age; she is very different from Amina, but very different. The woman is sitting on the floor on a carpet and she is breastfeeding her fourth child with a bottle. The brother, Adel, greets me, I know him, once Amina introduced us for a few seconds. Everyone is amazed to see me there at Adel house without warning. After the formalities, I explain that it would be advisable for Amina to leave him and his wife alone, that she no longer disturbs them with her presence. Then I add that I intend, indeed I have decided to hire her under my responsibility as a secretary for my studies at the university, briefly explaining the type of job I offer her. Amina would have turned eighteen after a couple of months. I am sure that the brother cannot refuse, I hold all the cards: they are all illegal immigrants, and it would be easy for me to insist and make him decide to let his sister go. In the meantime, Amina is silent; she stands straight in a corner with her eyes downcast. She doesn't dare challenge her brother, and luckily the other has just left for France. Adel initially disagrees to allow Amina to leave the house. I insist calmly and he replies to the point of almost causing a fight between him and me. We both manage to stay calm, until I see a different look on his face, almost like a smile, then he says to me: "Miss Sara, my sister is an income for my house, I wouldn't know how to do it without her help, you understand, we are refugees and we need money to survive, we have no assistance". Now I understood everything, I had the "go-ahead", but a bitter go-ahead; indeed, Amina suddenly looks up at Adel at these words, stares at him, with amazement and disappointment. I break the embarrassed silence and, without wasting time in useless discussions, I ask her brother how much he wants. He hesitates to figure out how much I'm willing to pay, then says a figure. I react violently and make it clear that they are all illegal immigrants and that Amina could lead a better life than she certainly expects in this house. Adel gets angry and sketches a violent arrogant reaction towards me, who in his eyes I'm just a woman. I'm not scared, I'm ready to punch him in the nose, and he understands my reaction, so he calms down like a coward. I make my move and offer a much lower amount than the expensive request before, but Adel resists. Eventually, after endless minutes, the "contract" is concluded. I grab Amina by the arm and drag her out almost against her will. She wanted to say something to her brother; she wanted to ask him if he ever loved her as a sister! I signal her to be quiet, not to waste time even in collecting her few things, and to follow me out of this house. We go out into the cool evening air, but we are both not as happy as we should be. Amina collapses to the ground crying, she is shocked and surprised by the reaction of her brother. She realizes that there were no family ties between them. I, on the other hand, fear I have slipped into something bigger than myself. Anyway, we are young; the world is ahead of us and awaits us. After this initial bewilderment, our life in my home resumes with days that are more peaceful. Amina is at home doing nothing, my salary is enough for me and for her, so better if she relaxes and recover from the bad treatment received by Adel. He considered her a bargaining chip, treated her like a stranger: I promised her brother a sum of money every month for a few months. In the meantime, our love is enough for us to live. Of course, we cannot lead a comfortable life, but we are happy, we are together at home. I realize that I am attached to her, and every day we understand more and more that we are a real family, even if not legally recognized. We don't exist for society, and I think about this refugee girl, she has gone from one hiding place to another: our life as a hidden couple. In the morning she is always the one who gets up first, I stay crouched in the bed and am happy to hear her whistling almost continuously as she prepares breakfast. Amina is used to whistling almost continuously as she does any activity throughout the day. I ask her "But how did you work in the pub without whistling?" She answers "I was whistling in my head ..." We love each other; we are one flesh and one soul.

One day, towards the end of my PhD year in Palermo, I would say casually and at the right moment, I receive an email from my former professor. He tells me that, having moved to Florence for an important position at the Superintendence of Fine Arts, he would like me to join him and help him. He offers me a permanent position for the next five years. I talk about it with Amina, and we are both enthusiastic, we finally move away from her brother. I accept the proposal of my former professor. In complete agreement, we gladly decide to move to Florence. Until the day of the departure, Amina no longer went to visit her brother, she is afraid of his wickedness, and then her sister-in-law has always shown all her dislike for Amina. The evening before departure, with all our belongings already packed, we decide to go to Adel's house together. We introduce ourselves shortly after dinnertime, when we know that her brother, having a full stomach, is able to think more calmly. We ring the intercom, he answers, and I, "Hi, I'm Sara, Amina is with me too". Silence.... Then he invites us to enter. He is surprised, he agreed on all the money, so he wonders what we do there! We go in and do not even say goodbye to the useless wife. We don't sit down, and he realizes that something is about to happen. Immediately, without wasting time, I explain to him that we are about to leave for Florence. Adel, "In Florence? Do you want to take my sister away forever? Never. Without my consent Amina does not move from this city", and I, approaching him almost speaking to his face," Amina is of age and she does what she wants. I have to move to Florence and she, being my secretary, has to come with me". Adel gets irritated and nervous, "No, my sister stays with me; she is a part of my family. How I justify her departure, what do I tell our parents?" I too, begin to get angry, "She is not part of your family and you sold her. Tell your family what you want, I don't care. Maybe you share with them the money I gave to you". I decide to leave and go to the front door taking Amina by the arm, but Adel stands in front of me to prevent me from going out, he insists that Amina does not go out this door. I don't give up, looking him straight in the eye and showing aggression, I tell him, "Get out of the way, step aside if you don't want me to hurt you. We go where I want". Holding Amina's slender arm tightly, I notice that the girl is trembling more and more, so I decide to push her hard towards the door to shake her, in the meantime I make my way pushing away Adel with my body, despite fearing a violent reaction from him. He takes me from behind by my jacket, but I push Amina towards the door screaming and calling him criminal. At my scream, the youngest child becomes frightened, feels a violent action and begins to cry. At the same time, that dull wife also utters a cry, almost an alarm for her husband, as if she wanted to warn him to stop and not go beyond it, for heaven's sake. Adel decides to leave me, while he looks at me with a look full of anger. I don't waste time; I open the door and push Amina out. Up until this point Amina was a little groggy, but as soon as we get out, as we go down the stairs of the building, she recovers and wants to go back and yell at her brother. I brake and I point out that it's okay, we won, we leave forever. We return home exhausted by strong emotions and by the fear of having been almost attacked. After dinner, we stay embraced lying on the sofa, planning our future. I light some scented candles and play soft, light music. We fall asleep sweetly.

The next day we both wake up rested. We get ready, take our bags, and take everything down, where a van should pick us up to take us to Florence. We are both still in tension, but none of us reveals it to the other; we both fear Adel may come with a knife to avenge her runaway sister.

Finally, the white van arrives. Two sturdy guys get out of the vehicle, apologize for the delay and go up with me to take the few little furnishings I have accumulated in the beautiful southern capital. While I'm in the apartment, I gasp, "What if that wretch man arrives just now that Amina is alone on the street?". I run down, and as soon as I leave the building, I find Amina in front of me who looks at me surprised with her big wide eyes, she asks me, "What happened?". I calm her down and hug her tightly, I don't care about the others, I hug my love tightly in front of everyone. Once the van is filled, Amina and I sit in a small space. Our journey into our new life begins.

During the trip, the two men, young and handsome, certainly strong, do their best to play the cockerel with us, and we indulge them. They ask us why we move and if we live together, we, to have fun, invent a strange and absurd story for our move to Florence. The two are so gullible that we can say anything without being caught. On the other hand, they are just coming on to us, with only the effect of making us laugh; we observe from above their masculine naivety. Kilometer after kilometer, with this old van the journey becomes tiring, the van seems to proceed at a snail's pace. During the trip, I am busy with various phone calls to receive the keys of the new rented house, and to organize the first meeting with my former professor. Amina keeps repeating that she is enthusiastic and that in Florence she will start a new job; she hopes to have a contract to become a regular worker in Italy. Everything has an end, and this journey on the back of a turtle is also over; we arrive late in the evening, tired. The two cockerels unload everything by transporting the little furnishings to the new house, which fortunately is located on the ground floor. They ask for more money or maybe wink at something else at the last minute: it is not clear what more they would like. We send them away mercilessly, tired of a whole day with the two guys so busy conquering us, that they didn't even notice the sweet glances that Amina and I exchanged. The house is beautiful and spacious with large windows facing the street. Opposite there is a local garden, so no prying eyes from other apartments and the windows are quite high from the sidewalk; despite being a ground floor there are five steps that raise it from the street. We decide to wash ourselves quickly and go out to have dinner. We are also excited because now my salary will be considerably higher; we could live with more serenity and above all Amina will be able to find a new job without haste. We feel fulfilled and serene now that we are a family, even if not legalized; no one can separate us. As I am at the counter to order dinner, I notice that Amina is writing something on a paper napkin. Well, I think she is compiling the list of things to buy! I go back to the table and as I sit down, I see that she has folded the paper, hiding it in my napkin. I know the paper is there, and she too knows I saw it while she hid it. However, I keep doing the comedy: I pretend I want to use the napkin, I open it and I uncover the paper. I read it and discover that she has written only two words, indeed two personal pronouns separated by a comma: "*YOU,*

ME". I look at her and she explains: "The shortest poem in the world is *'You and me'*, but now this is the shortest." I squeeze her hand tightly; I can't do anything else in front of people and I reply: "We will keep this note to remind us of this important moment". We'd like to kiss, but we're not allowed, so she's holding my hands in hers. At least this gesture can be mistaken for a gesture of friendship, even if a little excessive. The next morning, we get up late, we are tired of the journey and the transfer. We actually decide to stay in bed at least until lunchtime; we don't want to start working right away. Instead, today is Saturday, and no one will disturb us until Monday, which is when I have to meet my former professor. Lying in bed, we talk and remember the days gone by, the days when she worked and I was her client at the bar. In the meantime, we look around to decide which jobs to do first; for example, Amina decides to paint the bedroom first, and on one wall she wants to paint 'YOU, ME', large, so that it takes up most of the wall. She can do what she wants, as long as she doesn't involve me too; I'll be busy with work soon. We are lying talking about the shortest poem in the world written the night before and now resting on the bedside table. We are so tired that we don't even have the strength to have sex. In the afternoon, the first hectic activities begin. We draw up a list of the things we need, and Amina immediately goes to buy some of them; fortunately, there is a hardware store near the house. In the meantime, I start cleaning first, and then sorting out our things. While I work, I hear a whistle coming from the street: "e - C - - A A g - C - - ", tune that I then learned well. I don't pay attention to it, I tirelessly clean and clean, but that tune continues, then it occurs to me that it could be someone who wants to disturb. When I reach the window ready to react violently to any assault or harassment, I see a shadow hiding. Damn, I think, this is the downside of living on the ground floor. I lean out more and more irritated and I see a figure hidden behind the corner of the front door. She is Amina, luckily, I recognize her; I immediately suspected that Adel had discovered us. Is that girl playing a joke on me? I think about it for a while and then I whisper in a low voice from the window, "Come on, dear, my girlfriend Amina is not here, but we can have sex soon, she could be back at any moment". Amina hearing these words, bends down and looks at me with two big wide eyes; she wanted to play a joke, on me! Unfortunately, I start laughing, and the joke ends there. Amina carries a bag full of stuff, very heavy for her. We are in our house, the first house where we live free without her brother to disturb us. That weekend remained in our memories as if it were the party after a wedding, indeed it was not: we cannot officially marry both to the State and to society. The week starts with a lot of commitment for me: I start my work with enthusiasm, but as always when starting a new job there is still a lot of stress. Amina tries to encourage me and make sure she provides everything at home. The girl took care of the painting and cleaning work, she had to call the plumber for some minor adjustments. In the following days we went together to buy some small furniture, necessary for our few things. In the evening, usually, when I come back tired and exhausted, she makes me find dinner ready. As usual, the table is always decorated with many small-lighted candles, so many that it prevents me from handling the dishes, glasses and bottles without being burned. One evening, returning home, I find her excited and cheerful, she has a surprise, she announces that she has found a job. "But Amina, you don't want to rest a little first! You worked a lot for the house, and then there is no urgency, my salary is enough for both of us", and Amina: "I managed to find a job as a waitress, and unfortunately in black, but this time the owner has promised that he will hire me with a regular contract after an initial trial period". And I, " I think I can imagine what that pig wants when he asks for a probationary period!", Amina, "No, he's a good person, he asked me a lot of information about me and my life, and I preferred to confess everything, I didn't hide anything". Amina has always been a little naive and has always trusted strangers a lot. I answer, "Some men get aroused more with two lesbians, don't you know?", then she, "Calm down Sara, I need that work, I want to be with you and not depend on you". "Okay, when do you start?", "Tomorrow", "So quickly! Well, I'll accompany you, so I too can be sure that this man is not a pervert pig, and then let's see if he regularizes you or not, it would be nice if you could get a residence permit". Amina agrees, but she doesn't want to waste time with further chatter, she just wants to make Sara happy. She takes her hand and shows the table set with only seafood, as Sara likes it. They dine quickly; they don't even finish it because they are both already on the floor under the table clinging together as if it were their first time. They stay like this for hours, experiencing sexual pleasure many times, like never before. This renewed sexual understanding unites them and spurs them more and more to face the problems of an external world that has no room for them. The next day I take her to work, even if I skip my working day; luckily, my boss knows everything about me and understands my situation, indeed, he asks me to contact him for any problem. Finally, Amina and I arrive at the bar, a place, actually very nice and large with many waiters. Amina goes straight into the office and I with her. She knocks on the door and as soon as we are told to enter, we are faced with a lively old man, very jovial and friendly looking. Amina introduces me, and the owner gestures to get up while shaking my hand. Anyway, I'm a bit impetuous, and I start right away, without making him speak first. I ask him to explain Amina's working conditions and I make him understand that behind the girl there is me, and not only me, but also the director of the Superintendence where I work. The owner is happy to meet me and to learn this news; indeed, these are all good references for him. He confirms that he intends to regularize Amina, but that first he wants to take her for a shorter or longer trial period. He explains to me that putting the girl in a position to work at full capacity and to offer her a regular contract costs him a lot, so Amina has to start settling down for a first period of work. I am satisfied with this meeting and I too begin to relax a little; I leave Amina at work and go home. Her shift starts at 9.00 and ends at 18.00. She feels comfortable at work, even if she is busy all day, at least she starts a job that gives her the opportunity to be regularized with a residence visa. On my way home, I take a longer detour; I want to buy her a nice dress, a dress that is feminine: she always wears baggy pants and anonymous T-shirts. I choose an expensive shop where I buy a nice dress for the late afternoon, one with a dark blue background and small flowers abstractly drawn with various shades of yellow, but drawn in such an abstract way, that at first glance I thought they were colorful stars on a twilight sky. As soon as I get home, I hide it under her pillow. Tonight, I don't want to cook, I decide to go out for dinner as soon as Amina gets back from work. While I am lying and dazed with my eyes fixed on the television, but without following any program, I hear the tune, the usual one, whistling from the street: "e - C - - A A g - C - - ", Is she? It's only 3pm! I get up and go to welcome her happy, she probably finished her first day of work soon! I open the door a little worried, I hope that everything went well and that she is happy. I find her radiant for her first day at work; we hug each other in front of the door, regardless of passers-by and neighbors. She bought dinner at an expensive oriental restaurant; maybe she wants the evening to be more important. I make her a drink, so Amina begins to tell me, without interrupting, her first exciting work experiences. I think, "How can she be so enthusiastic if she was only a few hours at the bar!". We have dinner with the oriental food that she has brought, and after dinner, I take her by the hand and we go to bed, we will think about putting everything tidy tomorrow. She lingers in the bathroom, and when she reaches me, she is completely naked, she is so enthusiastic about her work, that she wants to amaze me even sexually.... naive doe, would you like to amaze me sexually...? After several stunts, I try to get her attention to the package under the pillow rather than me, when she finally finds the dress. She opens it with curiosity and is surprised, silent. I ask her if she likes it, and she replies with a weak "yes". I know very well that she will never wear it, I have never seen her wearing a women's dress. Amina, to get out of this awkward situation, has the good idea of wearing the dress with nothing underneath. She then approaches me as if it were the first time, as if we had just met. I support her, but while we're having sex, I don't mind biting her and intentionally hurt her a little. I would like to punish her; I must always take the initiative.

The days pass peacefully; I am more and more busy with my new job, which indeed goes good far beyond all expectations. My former professor has almost become our friend, indeed he has already invited us a couple of times to his house, where he lives with his wife. They are an elderly couple with no children. We also invited them one evening, and it was the first time we had guests at our house. On the evening of dinner, I am a bit tense; I begin to prepare everything I need to cook, while Amina has gone to do the last shopping. After a while, "e - C - - A A g - C - - ", I'm going to open the door, she wants me to open the door, she doesn't open it with her key. She likes my loving welcome; as soon as she enters, we kiss and hug each other always, usually. The evening with the professor and his wife passed calmly, Amina was initially tense because it is still difficult for her to reveal herself as a couple in front of other people, at least with those who do not belong to our same sexuality. She comes from a different mentality than ours. That evening at dinner, we were proud to be a family recognized by another family. After that dinner, with the passing of the days, we know and make friends with a colleague of mine; just today, we go out with him for a dinner outside the home. Amina doesn't seem very happy with this new friendship; she suspects that he looks at me not as a friend. I noticed her attitude, and I figured it was only due to her jealousy, she probably suspects that my colleague is flirting with me. While we get ready, she is in the bathroom, and when I take the dress lying on the bed, I discover a sheet folded in two. I am amazed; I open it and find another poem signed by Amina. Sometimes I think I should explain to her that I really don't have a talent for poetry. What a hassle, well, thank goodness it's short, let's read it:

'You blossomed like a flower,

and I,

I just caught your smell

so as not to fade your beauty '.

What a fool she is, I think, she has not yet learned and understood that we are indivisible, she still does not believe in my fidelity! The moment I am absorbed in these thoughts, something peeps into my mind…. "My fidelity …? Mmmmm, it would be a bit like being in jail … Oh well, I made a very bad consideration". In the meantime, Amina comes out of the bathroom, wearing that blue flowered dress that I bought her and that she only wore once. I'm sure she wears it again to show herself more attached to me: the jealous one. I look at her, smile at her, put her on the bed and we have sex; that dress with the blue background excites me. We arrive late at the restaurant, and we are surprised when my colleague Carlo introduces us to his new friend: Marianna. I'm sure she is more than just a friend, so suddenly I ask him brazenly, "What a nice surprise? Such a beautiful girl, I hope she is more than a friend to you…!" Carlo, looking Marianna in the eyes, replies that they have only recently met, and that some things have to mature. Okay everyone sees that they are in love, so I take the initiative and celebrate their meeting, indeed, we also celebrate our new friendship: Us as an occult family and they as an open couple.

The months go by, and the days go by quickly. In our little house, Amina and I feel like little birds in a nest; fortunately, Amina's family is a distant memory. Then comes the good news: the pub manager regularizes Amina. Finally, she too can live in Italy, no longer risking being discovered without a residence permit; she starts the procedures to obtain the residence permit. We are both over the moon. Now that we can travel, we plan to take a trip to England, where I was born and where I have lived since my teenage years. In short, everything seems to be fine. However, good days can be disturbed by a small cloud on the horizon; a cloud that everyone fears could turn into a storm. One Sunday morning, while we are having breakfast at home, Amina, evidently excited by our comfortable and happy life, reveals to me a project that perhaps she had been preparing from some time: "Why don't we organize a trip to the other side of the Mediterranean, just to visit my mother and my sister?". I am amazed, I did not expect it from her, and indeed, I am shocked. We are a fragile couple by the nature of our union, we have no legal ties between us and something unpleasant could happen to us considering the treatment received from Adel. I answer that perhaps it would be risky for two single women to expose themselves on a trip, certainly not a tourist one, on the other side of the Mediterranean, "Remember that your brother let you go almost reluctantly, only for the money. In case we go to your family in your Country, your brother will surely do something against me and also against you". Despite this Amina insists; she has a great desire to see her sister again, of whom she has not heard from since she left Adel's house in Palermo. We had decided not to communicate with her family so as not to leave a trace of where we moved. Amina perseveres in her project, and this is enough to make me understand that she misses her sister and mother very much, "Well, I tell her, let's think about it and try to organize ourselves to make this journey without running any risk". She hugs me, but this hug is a cause for concern for me. Then I think of Carlo and Marianna; they could escort us; it would be more appropriate to go with a man and not two women alone. The following days Amina continues her life in a more euphoric and happy way. Until now, I did not know, I did not imagine that she missed her family so much, or at least part of it. Other weeks go by without her talking about her project, which in my opinion is always a bit risky. Amina seems to stop insisting, probably she has second thoughts or perhaps she silently keeps this desire in her heart. One evening, as always, I am on the sofa reading reports relating to my work, when I hear, "e - C - - AA g - C - - ", I get up to open it as usual between us and, once I open the door, I see a paper note on the floor with a number written on it. I look around but do not see her, until as soon as I kneel to take the paper note; Amina comes out and jumps on me. Actually, she hurts my back a little, but I don't say anything. She is more euphoric than usual, she enters the house jumping for joy, while I, with the paper in hand, struggle to recover in an upright position. She asks me, " Guess who this number belongs to?" and I, seeing an international prefix and a very long number, "How did you find your parents' phone number?", and Amina "I went to the consulate of my Country. I explained that I wanted to get back in touch with my parents. First, they wanted to call my home to realize that there was nothing wrong with this. I have a regular residence permit for which I was not afraid of anything. Someone answered the call from the consulate, it was definitely my father, I heard a male voice. The official spoke briefly with this person and then they hung up the communication. He did not pass his interlocutor to me on the phone, so I assumed was my father who answered. I'm sure my dad wiped me out of his life and refused to talk to me!" As she concludes her story, she hugs me almost as if she wants to cry. I reply a little bitterly, actually quite nervous, "I told you not to get in touch with them, I understand that you are homesick, but you have to be careful. I would have addressed your sister or your mother first, but not certainly your father ... I know your mentality over there ... ". Amina separates from my embrace; I understand that she is offended. I try to comfort her, and I apologize, "I'm sorry, I meant that fathers are always a little stricter than mothers. Do you know what we do now? Let's call together and ask for your sister", and she, "But surely my brother or my father will answer", and I exhausted, "Then enough, let's not call. Let's close this story here". If Amina is disappointed, what can I do? What idiocy to resume contact with a family that certainly would not accept her anymore. The evening ends badly, we have dinner without talking to each other and go to bed ignoring each other. The next day everyone goes to work without even saying goodbye. I'm tired of pulling her like a wagon without tow, I'm tired of having to put up with her nonsense. While I'm home in the late afternoon, still mad at her, from the street I hear, "e - C - - A A g - C - - ", She is no longer mad with me. I go to open the door and find on the ground a basket full of red roses with very long stems. I call her and ask her to come out from the hiding place; I tell her that she should have not bought these roses. She slowly comes out from her unlikely hiding place and hugs me. Those few roses were enough to make peace, despite her imprudent desire to make that journey, a desire I cannot ignore. Overall, I can't object that much, so I decide to collaborate and organize her phone call to her home, and then also the visit to her Country. Better, not leave her alone to organize everything. After the basket of red roses, our life resumes without any particular novelty, maybe it's just she who is more and more anxious! Now she is increasingly busy working in the pub, where she has made many friends, as she claims. I warn her, and I repeat that those she meets in the pub are probably not real friends, but only people she deals with because they are customers of the pub. Sometimes, to test me, she tells me there is someone who is courting her. However, I don't believe her! She only has eyes for me, unfortunately. I am the one who feels imprisoned, I would like to disconnect from time to time, having other sexual experiences.

It has been about three years since we moved to Florence. One evening, while I'm always on the sofa resting after a busy day at work, I hear the usual "e - C - - A A g - C - - ". This time I really don't want to continue with this ritual, I don't get up to open the door. Amina whistles again until, not seeing me coming, she opens the door and silently approaches the sofa looking at me as if I had hurt her. Immediately I regret having treated her badly by not running to open the door. To recover, I conceive an excuse on the spot, to justify myself I give her a sop just to make her forget my behavior, "You know what? I think it's time to call your parents. When you whistled, I was on the couch absorbed in these thoughts". At these words of mine, she immediately lights up with a beautiful smile and hugs me, but I gently push her away from me, now I don't want her. Yes, I am despicable; I always knew I was. The point is that I met a woman at work, a guest of our office in Florence, who came for a conference. She is about ten years older than I am, I think. This woman intrigues me a lot; she is so feminine, well dressed in perfect hair and a handbag of the same color as the shoes. If I'm not mistaken, she sends signals to me too, but it's hard to tell. Meanwhile, I do nothing but think about her body and the desire I have to kiss her. Amina is my woman, but that lady turns me on a lot. In the following days, I can hardly have sex with Amina, surely, she noticed my behavior, but I justify it by saying that I am in tension for this demonized phone call with her family. This professor would be leaving in a few days, so I have little time; I have to hurry to understand if she likes me. Amina on her part, seeing me so tense, she almost thinks it's better not to make the phone call anymore, and she tells me to forget the matter of her family, since all this causes me so much stress. I understand that I can no longer go on, one morning I decided to change things quickly, I call her family to give her a cuddle and then also to distract her attention from me. I want to be the first to speak, in case the father or brother answered. The phone rings, we are both tense, until a woman answer who I think says something like "Hi", well, it's a female voice, so I immediately hand the phone to Amina. She doesn't speak immediately, she waits a few seconds until the woman, on the other side, repeats "Hello", only now Amina recognizes her sister, and greets her with a weak, shy voice. The woman on the other side is silent, but after a few seconds, she calls her by name: "Amina", and cries. Amina cries too, and then they both start a conversation in their language that I don't understand at all. They both look very happy, and the tears never stop flowing down Amina's face. After a few minutes, I leave the room and quickly and secretly send a message to the beautiful professor, while Amina greets her sister; she is happy and radiant. She tells me that her sister really answered, as I suspected, and that her family misses her very much, but that they could not contact her because Adel had reported that Amina disobeyed the rules of the family and that she lives who knows where and who knows how. Her mother and sister, more than her father, were very anxious about her, and believed that she was now lost. During the phone call, the two sisters promised to set up a meeting, and Anbar, this is her sister's name, would speak with the mother and father to try to rehabilitate Amina for the whole family. Amina explained to her that she lives with a friend of hers and she works regularly leading a quiet and comfortable life. There is a new air in the house: Amina is busy with her pseudo friends at the pub and is excited about seeing her family again. Therefore, I'm free to go and conquer the beautiful professor, who unfortunately will leave in a couple of days. I rush to her hotel to take my chances. As soon as I arrive, I'm tense, the doorman warns her of my visit, and she begs him to let me up to her room. Wooowwww, while I'm in the elevator, my heart is beating fast. I arrive at her door, I fix my hair a little and I also fix my breasts, a little higher, then I knock. I hear her voice inviting me to enter. As soon as I enter, I look around and immediately see her sitting in an armchair with her hair always perfectly gathered, a black dress not very low-cut and long up to below the knee, with a pair of black velvet shoes, a pearl necklace and a huge ring sparkling on the finger. She smiles at me and begs me to sit in the chair next to her. I am confused, I don't know what to say, I don't know how to justify my visit, I don't know ... I don't know how to transcend the rules of the society to which we are subjected. She smiles calmly, surprises me and offers me a glass of the same drink, I don't know what it is, I don't even care to know. As soon as she hands me the glass, this sophisticated middle-aged woman touches my hand, which I reached out to take the glass. I have a thrill, is it an invitation or am I still wrong? Can I make a clearer advance? On the other hand, do I still have to stay in my place? What a scandal if I ask her to allow me to kiss her, and in response, she sends me away in horror. Absorbed in these thoughts I don't realize that we are both mute. She, from the height of her experience, understands that she is in an advantageous position, and surprising me: "Please, excuse me;

I was preparing to take a bath". I don't answer, my tongue has disappeared down my throat. The elegant lady, without waiting for my answer, gets up and as she goes towards the bathroom, in a way I would say more than chancy, unzips her dress, until, reaching the bathroom door, she takes it off and drops it on the floor. I'm amazed, she took me away from all embarrassment. I see her, just for a moment, covered, or uncovered, only by transparent underwear, as black as the dress she took off. She then disappears into the bathroom without turning to me. I don't know what to do, I'm still hesitant, but driven by a primal instinct I get up, reach the bathroom door and shamelessly lean on the door jamb sipping my drink. She is sitting on the edge of the tub, intent on filling it. She smiles at me; I respond with a smile that badly hides my desire for her. Enough, I approach, I reach out to untie her hair, but she stops me, she unties them while she gets up. She goes behind me and puts her hands on my shoulders giving me a light massage. That's enough, I turn my head to kiss her hand, and she doesn't pull it back, so I take her and kiss her. She responds with more feeling than I do. We fall to the floor in the bathroom and there we consume our ardor. There on the bathroom floor we remain for hours in convulsive movements of love. There is no longer well-groomed hair, elegant clothes, and precious pearls; there are two naked bodies gently fighting for sex. My cell phone rings, I recover, it's 4.30 pm ... Damn Amina is back home, and she hasn't found me. I jump up, wash myself quickly in the tub of the lady, who is lying

on the floor watching me while I wash myself hastily to remove her smell from my skin. I dry quickly, while she wears a floor-length velvet robe, finally I get dressed faster than light. Then I stop; look at her, and she once again takes me away from the embarrassment: "Go, my dear, thanks for this nice surprise". We kiss each other and promise to meet again. I go out quickly and look for a plausible excuse for Amina; I do not know what to say. I call Carlo: "Carlo please you have to cover me. I did something I can't explain and now I need an alibi for Amina. I went to the professor lady, our guest, in her hotel; I had some documents to give her". Carlo laughs, "In reality you are no different from us...! Oh well, I tell Amina that we have been busy in the office together because today the professor has to leave". "Well Carlo, thanks. Of course, we are the same, why shouldn't we be! Ok, that's a good excuse. Now I call Amina and reassure her. In five minutes, please call her too and ask if I have already arrived home, since we were late because of the professor and you wanted to talk to me about some work matters, so you can convince her of the reason for my delay". Carlo supports me and so we both do. Back home I find Amina totally persuaded by our apologies, on the other hand she is distracted by the emotion of having contacted her family again. I am calm and not at all regretful of what I did, indeed, since if it was so easy, I will do it again.
I just have to be more skilled not to be caught.

The journey.

After the adventure with the beautiful professor, our guest in the office, I must confess that I have had other stories. Two to be honest, I'm too afraid of getting caught. Amina has increasingly settled in Florence; knows many people and sometimes I don't want to go out with her and the last friends she thinks she has; it is difficult to consider someone a true friend. I am satisfied with my life and with my, or rather ours four or five truly friends. I am pleased that she is busy, both with her work and with her friends, so I have more time for myself, for my job that occupies me so much, but also for my lovers. I love Amina, but from my point of view, physical love shouldn't be exclusive. Why should that be? Amina comes from a fairly traditional mindset, and besides, everyone is made in their own way. She always comes back at the same time, she has never worked overtime, she is always regular in her affairs and above all, she always loves me very much. I too want it more than anything else. I am her light, as she says, and she continues to write me a poem from time to time, I don't even try to tell her to stop writing. Poems bore me, but by now, I've gotten used to her. Maybe I'm icy, I don't love her as much as I used to, I don't know! I just know that I like having my own secret space, but I wouldn't want her to suffer, she doesn't deserve it. A couple of times I forced her to go together to an LGBT club. She followed me as a faithful little dog follows her master, how selfish I have been. While we were in the club, she always sat without socializing with anyone, without dancing; at most, she had a drink. Later I realized that it would not be appropriate to return to these clubs, at least together. My idea of life is to have mistresses from time to time, and then we are not all the same. She is satisfied with a monogamous relationship; I am not. One evening on my way back from one of those clubs, I ask her clearly if she would like to have a triangle with another girl or with a couple of girls! She replies clearly and decisively that she would rather disappear and leave forever. Well, we go home and go to bed; we fall asleep without even a caress. The next day at breakfast, I feel a bit guilty for my behavior, so I decide to use my last trick up my sleeve. While we have breakfast sitting like two strangers in the kitchen, I ask her, "What do you think if we organized a visit to your parents' house?" and I add, "but calmly, trying to plan everything in detail!". She smiles in wonder, but afterwards she is saddened, "Do you want to give me up at my parents' house and leave!". She makes my heart explode; only now do I understand how many worries I have caused her with my stupid traitor attitude. I get up and hug her, "Silly, I would never let you go. You are mine and I am yours forever". The fool is moved and reassured; we both know, deep in our hearts, that some of us have told a half-lie.

Indeed, from that day on, our life is once again in fibrillation. She often talks to me about her parents describing their character, as well as their physical appearance, and then she describes her sister, the youngest of her home, Anbar, the one with whom she has a special bond. I can no longer listen to these stories that, in truth, interest me little. I was intrigued only the first and perhaps the second time she told me ... but enough is enough. Finally, we decide to make this trip with Carlo: I would have pretended to be Carlo's sister and Amina's best friend, that is, the one who hosts her and gives her the opportunity to work and save money. We invite Carlo and Marianna home for a dinner on a Friday night, we start our home evening happily, we are very close-knit. From the beginning of the evening Amina cannot wait and immediately starts the discussion on the trip. Carlo seems to be happy, Marianna a little less, probably does not like to feel excluded from the project. When I notice her bad mood, I give a turn to the organization, immediately deciding on a different coverage for our trip. I will be Carlo's sister and Marianna his wife. Amina intervenes, "Sorry but how can you be Carlo's sister if you have a different surname?". We remain stunned, and then I reply, "I keep the surname of my husband who died, and since I am still in love with him, I have not changed his surname to mine". Well, it all seems organized. Now it remains to fix the date of departure, respecting the commitment of all of us, therefore, not having coincident dates, it is necessary to update ourselves in a few days because of our commitments. As I imagined, we all have different days of holidays, our commitments do not coincide, but after a few joints and a few moves, we decide that the date would be May, in about a month. By the way, in May it will be six years since Amina and I have met. Well, everyone is satisfied, especially Amina who will finally see her family again. I hide from her my strong fears about how her father will react! Siblings living abroad have only told lies to their parents just to put Amina in a bad position. Especially Adel, the brother of Palermo, that of the horrendous request for money to let his sister go, especially he slandered his sister more. As Anbar revealed to us, Brother Adel told the family that Amina had left without his permission, going to live elsewhere with a friend of her, and that he tried in vain to prevent her. Perhaps Adel, feeling guilty towards the family for letting her go in exchange for money, will also have invented a few more lies to his parents, as if Amina's terrible gesture of leaving alone was not enough. I don't know, I'm afraid that if we go there, they wouldn't let Amina go back to Italy with me. I'm afraid, so I decide to reveal these doubts to Amina. She seems not to lose her serenity, confirms that her parents are not as bad as her brother is and then she has a very good relationship with her sisters. Since she resumed communicating by phone with Anbar and her mother, both women have never mentioned bad information received from Brother Adel. Yes, according to her father she was wrong and lives against the rules of her society, since she lives alone, outside the family, without the presence of a man who is a member of the family. Finally, she assures me that she has also explained her version of events, starting with the bad coexistence she had with her brother, especially when his wife and children joined him. She believes she has managed to bring the women of the house to her side; however, no one knows the true feelings of the father towards her, he could also assert the right of parental authority on an adult daughter! I do not know the legislation of her Country, nor does Amina know it. I do not insist on not making her worry further, whatever happen, now Amina has a residence permit because she has an employment contract here in Italy. Since we decided to embark on this journey, our life has calmed down: I don't want to seek extramarital adventures, and Amina is too busy showing me her love and being kind and affectionate to me. In the evening, our ritual continues in a somewhat lightened way: when I hear the usual whistled tune, I do not rush to open the door, but I call her by name and greet her before she even opens the door. Sometimes I reach her at the door and we hug at the entrance not caring about others. By now we know our neighbors, almost all good people, of course, except for someone who does not admit these "relationships out of nature", as the owner of the third floor clearly told us. Maybe he hates us or maybe he is intrigued by us! His wife left him a year ago taking their two children with her. Since he was alone, he does nothing but speak ill of women, and once, deliberately making himself heard by us, he said that women are unreliable and lesbians are worse. Amina is a bit scared of him, she is small in build, but I reassure her by telling her that if that racist tried to hurt us, I would beat him. One day I was forced to buy a large enough wooden rolling pin, with fixed handles, that is, carved in wood, so as to be more stable when I held it as a weapon. We keep it resting immediately behind the front door, ready for any eventuality, for any urgency. Even the elderly couple who live on the same floor as the racist, since they understood the type of relationship between Amina and me, have stopped speaking to us, they limit themselves to just greeting us. Indeed, the husband does not stop at the only greeting; the old man always gives us a smile when he meets us, without being seen by his wife. That kind of smile that makes us understand that he would gladly participate in a "love session" with Amina and me. Men sometimes, when they know we are lesbians, get excited. They tell us that they understand our sexual desires, they do not condemn us, unfortunately they add that they would like us to share our wishes with them "as nature commands"; at least that's what a pub customer told Amina, when he learned that she is a lesbian and that she lives with a woman. It is a daily struggle against ignorance and machismo. Unfortunately, if they were only racist, I would have weapons to fight, but against machismo, it would take a cultural revolution and not just a simple weapon. Some neighbors have now also noticed the signal between Amina and me when she returns home, the whistled tune. The student on the first floor, our almost friend, teases us by imitating the tune when she meets us in a playful and affectionate way. As a result, even the racist on the third floor knows it, probably.... I fear that he will come by imitating the whistle, making me

66

open the door to hurt us. Sometimes he is really irritable and aggressive. However, the rolling pin is always next to the front door. We are close to the date of departure. The plane tickets have been bought, the hotel booked, and finally Amina decides to call her sister to inform her of the trip. From her mobile phone she dials the long number ... we are waiting for someone to answer. I am very tense; I have no idea of her family's reaction. Luckily, her sister answers the phone; father and mother are out for shopping. Amina informs Anbar, speaking in her mother tongue, and I, not understanding anything, try to sense something from her expression and tone of voice. They talk and talk; I get bored and I go away to get something alcoholic to drink: I require it. Finally, the phone call ends, but only because, as Amina tells me, her parents are coming back. So what? I ask her in full suspense. She replies that the sister is very happy to see me again, logically, but fears for the reaction of the father. In any case, the sister suggested that she should not go to the hotel, it would not be good in the eyes of the neighbors, but she should sleep at her parents' house. Then she strongly suggested that for that occasion it would be better if she showed up wearing traditional clothes. Amina has to prove something more to the neighbors and above all in front of her father. Let us hope that everything goes well, I would not like to have to struggle with the social rules of that Country as well. I think it is better if I now turn to a lawyer or to someone who knows the rules and legislation of that country. I would like to know if a kidnapping of Amina is plausible and feasible, if her parents can forcibly oppose her return to Italy. I decide to take information secretly; I don't want to worry Amina further. A week later, just two days before departure, not finding any lawyer experienced in this field, I decide to go to the consulate of their Country. Unfortunately, a low-ranking official receives me since the consul is occupied, as well as the vice consul and the whole hierarchy above this official. The man, while listening to my story patiently, barely holds back a mocking smile, so much so that I am about to punch him in the face, before leaving, but I self-control and remain calm, waiting to listen what he has to say to me. Finally, after listening, he begins by stating that homosexuality is punished in his country and that Amina has violated family law, as well as committed the crime of homosexuality. That a woman like her is considered outlawed and that ... I don't want to listen to him further. I interrupt him, thank him and greet him, leaving him without listening to his answer or any greeting. Leaving the consulate, I realize that I have met someone who is little more than a door attendant, a fool who gave me his point of view, and not perhaps the real one of his Country. I was impulsive to leave without first waiting for someone more polite than he was, oh well, now the day after tomorrow we leave. I do not say anything to Amina about my visit. On the day of departure, we are all a bit tense, maybe only Marianna is not. Anyway, I do everything to distract Amina, but I can do very little, indeed, she often goes to the bathroom to pee, as always when she is tense. During the flight Amina participates little in our talks, she is immersed in other thoughts, and we all understand that she tries to imagine how much her parents have changed and what her first meeting with them will be like. She has not seen them for about seven years, when I met her, she had already been in Palermo for a year, plus the six years since we live together in Florence. We land. We head silent to take our luggage, no one wants to talk, and the emotion has taken all of us. At the exit of the airport, I have a nasty surprise, we find Adel to welcome us. I'm terrified, that bad guy rushed here too; he definitely has a plan in mind. Frightened beyond all limits, I take Amina by the arm making her understand that I do not intend to leave her alone in his hands. Amina has no reaction, while Carlo and Marianna do not understand, but they feel my tension. Adel justifies his presence by explaining that he was forced by his parents to come to pick up Anima at the airport: they have to show to the neighborhood that Amina lives in Italy with him and that therefore she came with her brother visiting her parents. I don't believe it, but that fool of Amina does not rebel and does not imagine that it could be a deception. I decide to turn directly to Adel, and looking at him menacingly in his eyes, "Maybe you did not understand, where Amina goes there, I go too" and he: "Come on, what problem is there? You come in the car with us, but Amina, she sleeps in her house". "Well, I answer, It means that you will have to fix a bed for me too", and Adel: "No, it is not possible, you came with your brother and his wife and stranger men are not allowed in our house, my last little sister is looking for a husband and will most likely get married next year. No man outside the family can sleep in my parents' house". I don't know what to do, at the moment we all get into the car; the brother is silent while loading our luggage. I am tense, but very tense. During the journey in the car no one speaks, except the brother who instructs us on how to behave and what to say in case we talk to the neighbors. Finally, he pulls out a typical local coat and forces Amina to wear it, which she does without replying, as agreed before. We cross the city center cutting it on an elevated highway, until we arrive in the first suburbs, in an area with all low houses surrounded by high walls of pure white color, on which stand out the wooden doors sometimes blue and sometimes faded wood color. The streets are curved but also wide enough to let two cars pass at the same time. Few people on the street. We arrive in front of one of the doors; this is blue with a door clapper that looks like brass. Adel parks very close to the wall, so much so that we leave the car all on the opposite side of the wall. As we get out of the car, we don't see anyone around, not even a passerby, but Adel still hurries to unload Amina's luggage. Then he immediately knocks with the door clapper, but with little force, as if he did not want to alert the neighbors as well. The door opens, we do not see who opened it, and we only glimpse a hand that makes us the gesture of entering. Adel pushes us to hurry, and we crowd a little confused; we seem to be like spies in a movie. Just inside we are in front of a large courtyard, all whitewashed and shining with white, so much so that the sun, reflecting on its walls, dazzles us. The one who has just opened the door captures my attention: a woman wrapped in veils, an elegant figure, small in build like Amina, could be the mother, even if she seems too youthful. She has a beautiful amber skin and the few jewels she wears of pure yellow gold, stand out on her skin highlighting the charm of the woman. At first, no one introduces us to the beautiful woman; indeed, we all enter the house without saying a word yet. Only once inside the house, Amina rushes to embrace the woman who opened us, calling her mom. In the room, another young girl is anxiously waiting; she too is very similar to Amina, small in build with curly hair, perhaps more than Amina's. She, too, has uncontrolled tears running down her beautiful cheeks. After the long greeting with her mother Raissa, the two sisters finally embrace. She is Anbar, Amina's last sister, the one who spoke by phone with Amina in recent months and as announced by Adel, the one who must marry in about a year. After the greetings between the women of the house, they introduce us to both; the mother offers me the gentle and elegant hand like her whole figure. Anbar asks us if we are thirsty, if we need to refresh ourselves. She expresses herself in a perfect French, and we, as Italians, can understand her quite well. While they serve us a mint drink in the entrance room, which I see is also a dining room and living room, they explain that Amina's father is about to return and that we will therefore have lunch on his return. We women all go to the room intended for us and refresh ourselves. Carlo, in spite of himself, remains alone with Adel. After about an hour, we hear the door opening, it is the father. Amina is tense; all of us hurry back to the main room. Finally enters a man quite big and ungainly in his features, I would say very similar to his son. Adel rushes to introduce us, and he politely responds with a kind and embarrassed greeting. I notice that he is very shy and seems docile; his appearance does not resemble his character at all. Later in the day, I have the opportunity to ascertain that he is a quiet and peaceful man. Unfortunately, he did not deign Amina even a glance, but we all glimpsed a strong emotion in him. At lunchtime, the sister invites us to go to the kitchen, where we find the food prepared for us women, while Carlo remains at the table with Adel and his father, constantly and lovingly served by Anbar and Raissa. Marianna can also have lunch with Carlo and the others. Carlo and Marianna attempt a protest explaining that they would like everyone to have lunch at the table, but Amina herself makes them desist. In the end it is better this way, I get to be alone with the women of the family and get to know them better. That unfortunate Carlo and Marianna, forced to eat with two strangers, however I realize that they immediately make friends with both, at least I feel that almost Carlo flows serenely with them, perhaps more with Adel than with the father for language problems. After lunch we stay in our rooms because both the group of women, to which Amina's mother is finally added, and the group of men, take a siesta, indeed it is a moment during which we start a less formal conversation. Marianna joined us, and we actually witness Amina's long talks with her mother and sister, they had not seen each other for years, and we decided to stay a little on the sidelines so as not to disturb them. I am pleased to see Amina finally relaxed and enjoy her family, just enough to make me relax too. However, as all chickens come home to roost, so it comes time to go to the hotel. In an unscrupulous and perhaps rude way, I ask Mother Raissa directly if I can sleep there with them. The woman is silent, evidently, she cannot consent, instead Adel intervenes immediately who, by his grace and my luck, agrees to let me sleep with them. I greet Carlo and Marianna, who warn me to ring on their mobile phone in case I find myself in trouble; a single ring would alert them and they would rush here right away. Finally, after this busy day we go to bed. I sleep in the same room with Amina and Anbar, the brother in another room and so do the parents. Not trusting yet, I make sure to place my mattress on the ground near the door, I want to watch over anyone who came in or out during the night. Amina fell asleep very late because she and her sister were talking quietly all the time, sometimes giggling. I, although I want to be vigilant, fall tired in the arms of Morpheus, without even realizing it. In spite of myself, I wake up late in the morning, almost suddenly, still sleepy but rested. I find the room empty and I have a gasp, I go out abruptly and I come across, almost clash, with the two sisters while they happily go to the kitchen to have breakfast with their mother. The men of the house went out early in the morning for some of their business. I immediately phone Carlo and Marianna to reassure them, indeed Amina tells me to warn them that we are going to pick them up with Anbar to take them on a tour of the capital; then she added that their cousin and neighbor, Alif, would accompany us. During the few days of our stay, the time passes serenely: I still do not believe it. However, in the end everything is fine. Alif, Amina's cousin, is of the same age as her and has just started a job as a mechanical technician in a factory. He is pleasant and nice and above all, I realized that he is like another brother for Amina, but an acquired brother whom Amina loves very much, being also reciprocated. Anbar tells me that it would be time for her to choose a husband, her parents showed her some photos and she has already chosen one. She adds that, shortly thereafter, they would organize their first meeting, strictly in the presence of all four parents. I ask her if she loves him, and she candidly replies no, but the love must be desired and built over time. She is sure that it will come during the years of marriage. I think she is infatuated with this young man, known only in photos. She assures me that the parents will not decide the wedding date, until they first meet and until they have been dating for some time, always in the presence of their parents. The two young people must check, as far as possible I would add, if they were compatible. I'm sorry for Anbar, but she seems to be very happy. A small problem arises when the mother Raissa asserts that it is unusual for the last daughter to marry while Amina is still unmarried. Then she adds that they make an exception since Amina lives abroad with Adel and concludes that Adel will find her a husband among their people. The woman spoke emphatically, as if she were reading a perpetual proclamation. In truth, perhaps I am wrong, but I guess she wanted to warn me, regarding the certainty that one day Amina will DEFINITELY get married, and she will do so under the supervision of her brother. However, I remain silent; I do not say anything, I think that Amina will hardly return to visit her family. Finally, it's time to return to Italy. Amina hugs her mother and sister strongly, and they all cry. The father remains on the sidelines, and when we are already close to the door with luggage in hand, he nods Amina asking her to approach him. Amina goes to him fearful, he looks into her eyes, perhaps for the first time since the beginning of our stay, and then tells her something that I cannot understand. Amina is surprised, and then she thanks him happy and more and more moved reaches us, so we finally go out to get into the car driven by Adel. We leave to reach Carlo and Marianna at the airport, but shortly after leaving the parents' house, we meet Alif who was waiting for us along the way to say goodbye. Adel, however, stops just long enough for a short greeting, without allowing us to get out of the car. Both Amina and I are sad and disappointed for not having had the opportunity to greet that dear boy properly; however, Alif understands our regret and beckons us that everything is fine. We look at him backwards as he disappears further and further away. Adel notices our disappointment, and justifies himself by saying that there is no time, there is traffic to the airport. Only on the plane, Amina confides to me that her father gave her his blessing before letting her go, whatever she does. This unexpected blessing gave Amina a certain serenity for the future. Her father, the one who seemed to be the gruffest of the family, partially freed Amina from her position as a rebel. We both realize that Adel is the uncompromising of the family.

By now, a few months have passed since we returned home. Our life is resumed as always. Amina has regained her tranquility, as she was when I met her; she seems to have definitively re-established relations with her family. I am glad for her calm and loyal character, even if sometimes it bores me a little. Indeed, her loyalty as a couple worries me. I am always looking, even if not intentionally, for some adventure, while she is structurally always sincere and faithful. In the following months, I tried to induce her to go out more and more with her friends, usually the customers of the pub where she works. Therefore, I can spend a little more time alone; or rather, I met a girl. She recently arrived in Florence to take a tailoring course. I met her in the audience at a cultural event where my boss was a speaker. She approached me after the conference. She watched me while I spoke with the professors, at least so she confessed to me after. She waited for me to free myself and go to the bar counter to have something, any drink, useful to relax after the commitment and tension of the conference. I let her do it, in the sense that I gave her rope, but I did not intend to know her better, she threatened me. Afterwards we met a few times, always strictly before six in the evening, the time when I have to go home, that is, before Amina's return from work.

Since we returned to Florence, a couple of guys soon became very dear to both: Cristian and Cris. In truth, they both are called Cristian, but logically one of the two chose Cris. We became close friends since Cris was born in Italy, but his mother comes from a Country bordering Amina's native. Cris explained to us that, although he knows his mother tongue, in truth he has never been to his country; his mother moved with his family to Italy when she was just two years old. Refugee with her family; they no longer have relatives or ties in their home Country. Our circle of friends, the common ones between Amina, and me has expanded; we meet quite often, taking turns at the home of some of us. Carlo and Marianna got married just a year after our return, as well as Anbar, Amina's sister got married. We received the wedding invitation. One negative news overshadowed the good news of the two marriages: Amina is worried about the work; unfortunately, the owner of the pub has just given up the license. This change of management has brought agitation in our family ménage; Amina has become a bit taciturn, almost grumpy. She would have liked to be present at her sister's wedding, but at work, the new boss has reset the holidays and increased the hours of work.

Sometimes we fight for nothing and then for a couple of days we don't speak to each other. We spend at least a couple of months in this situation, and our friends have noticed this. They try to calm us down and comfort us, but despite them things seem to fall between Amina and me. After yet another quarrel, I scream at her to go to her country to her sister and not to bother me anymore with her sadness and apprehensions. She replies that the owner of the pub is not sure if she will find her job when she returns; indeed, he wants to put in order the financial balance of the pub, which, in truth, is not flourishing. The old owner was very good, often gave credit and even more often gave big extra tips to the most loyal employees, those who needed extra help. With the new owner the wind has changed, it seems that he wants to turn it into a bar for meetings between adults. Amina is increasingly nervous, and a wall of incommunicability has now been raised between us. One day, she returns from work strangely serene, for at least a couple of months, when she returns, she no longer announces herself with her usual whistled tune. As soon as she enters the house, she immediately warns me that she has decided to go and visit her sister, whatever it costs for her work, as she is just a waitress, she will find another job on her return. She also phoned her brother Adel, who suggested moving the trip to a month, the time to be able to free himself to accompany her. I don't offer to go with her, I keep pouting on her. Since that day the tension between us has subsided. I try to be as kind as possible to her because I fear something bad could happen if she really travels with her brother. I have a 'sixth sense' that warns me of something.

This month also passes during which I am anxious, while Amina bought the ticket, indeed, Adel bought it. She will leave by train from Florence to Palermo and from there they will take the plane together. She did not want to go by plane to Palermo; she said that in this way she has more time to think. The fateful day comes, I have a strange feeling, as if I were about to lose her, but I get strong, I smile at her and reassure her. Amina is serene, while I have the feeling of walking on hot coals. When I escort her to the train station, I regret how things have gone over the last few months, even though she was always short-tempered. I try to show her my concerns, not to ruin her party, but to make her understand that she needs to be more cautious on this journey without me. Amina smiles little, she is not entirely convinced of what she is doing, and at least, so it seems from her attitude. At the last moment, as the train moves to leave, I tell her, "Call Alif immediately as soon as you arrive, meet with him and ask him for help with any problem, indeed send me Alif's phone as soon as you can, so I can also communicate with him". Amina agrees and for the first time, after days, hints at a smile, but some tears flow on her face. Those tears make me very happy; they are our reconciliation and complicity. Thank goodness, she leaves and I'm a little quieter. I return home accompanied by a sense of guilt: for what fault? Maybe a lot. I realize that I have not been as faithful as she is to me, that I have often told her lies, finally because I have unknowingly expressed my impatience with her constant attention to me. Now! Now I let her go alone! I could have left too, but I'm stupid and maybe resentful. it's the first time we separate since we met in Palermo, and for this, I suffer even more. During the train ride, Amina often sends me messages via mobile phone. We both do not like to talk on the phone on the train: first, we disturb the other passengers and then there is no privacy at all. She manages to call me only when the train enters the destination station, she warns me that she does not know when she can call me again, but in any case, we will communicate through messages always and constantly. Now more than before I begin to be tense again. After about an hour she writes to me that she is at her brother's house and they are about to have dinner. The sister-in-law has not changed at all; indeed, perhaps she has worsened, does not speak to her and treats her coldly. I tell Amina not to pay attention to it; the unfortunate woman certainly suffers too: she must have sex with your brother and must submit to him for everything. Amina answers me with a series of smiling emoticons from cell phone. Well, at least I hope I made her smile a little. The night passes badly; I had several nightmares. As soon as I wake up, I immediately check if she sent me a message, fortunately I find some. She confirms to me that her night has passed quietly, and that her brother is preparing the luggage, in truth a lot of luggage, maybe he wants to bring many gifts to his parents! They will take the plane at 12.30. Afterwards she always updates me, punctually as soon as she goes somewhere or sees someone, and I reassure myself. Then a message from her, very short, in which she tells me that she is entering the plane. During her brief stop at her brother in Palermo, Adel is always there next to her, and if not her brother, the detestable sister-in-law. I didn't want to ask if they were controlling her more or less covertly, and for what purpose they do it. Well, better not to think about bad things, I tell myself.

I am particularly busy with my job, my boss is about to retire and does not want to leave me at the mercy of an uncertain future, the program I was carrying out is almost over. One day he summons me to his office, and he plans for me to move to Great Britain, to London. I am surprised, and my thoughts immediately go to Amina who is now far away, I cannot make a decision by discussing it with her first. However, he assures me that I don't have to decide right away, I have time to think about it. I inform him that Amina is now in her country visiting her family and he consoles and heartens me up, evidently, he has noticed that I am very tense. Amina continues to text me and sometimes call me. She wrote me the first message as soon as she left the destination airport. Then some very short messages up to the one in which she describes to me the meeting with her mother. A few more messages follow; in one of them, she tells me that she met Anbar's husband. She writes that he is a handsome boy, but she did not have the opportunity to speak privately with Anbar, to know if he is a good man or is despotic. Unfortunately, she has only been able to meet her sister once and does not understand why she cannot go to visit her whenever she wants! On the morning of the ninth day since she is with her family, as soon as I wake up, I immediately open the phone to read the latest messages, but I can't find any. She is obviously packing her bags, indeed the day after tomorrow she has to take the plane to return to Italy. It's already lunchtime, and nothing, no message. I don't want to worry yet, but I'm afraid, maybe she'll write to me as soon as she can. It's now evening, and still nothing. Now I start to send her messages, but I still do not receive any response, indeed I see that my messages are not even read in her mobile phone. Before going to bed, I also try to call her, but her phone is turned off or disconnected. Damn, she didn't even give me the phone of Alif, her cousin, at least I could call him. The next morning, I woke up before dawn, I slept little and I still had nightmares. No message from Amina. Now I'm really scared, it seems to me like I'm walking on the edge of an abyss. I don't know what to do. I decide to go to work, but only to distract myself and pass the time. Still no message, I go crazy. It's evening, I don't want to have dinner, my stomach is closed, I deceive myself thinking that maybe she has her mobile phone without charge or broken, and she doesn't change it because tomorrow she has the plane to go back to Italy! Tomorrow, she has to come back and the reckless one doesn't use any phone to reassure me! I pretend I don't know I've found the broken phone excuse just not to think the worst. These are terrible moments, all night I am completely awake, desperate for fear that something has happened to her. On the third day, that of her return, I wake up without any communication from her yet. In desperation, I decide to call Palermo airport to ask if Amina's flight is scheduled to be delayed, they tell me that no delay is expected. I ask how I can know the passenger names that have boarded! They tell me that it is not possible to have the list. I insist, but I understand that they cannot satisfy my request for privacy reasons. I wait for the time when the plane should land. An hour passes, then two, and always nothing, I do not receive any message from Amina. I still try to call her, but her phone is always off. I would like to cry, scream, I am desperate. Our friends are aware of everything; indeed, they call me often to comfort me. Four hours have now passed since the plane landed. I call the airport and they confirm that the flight landed on time. They can't tell me anything else about the passengers. I try to call the airline's office, but even they cannot reveal anything to me, out of respect for the privacy of passengers. This damn privacy. I do not waste any more time, it is useless to stay in Florence, I decide to take the car and rush to Palermo. I want to go directly to Adel's house. Unfortunately, no one can come with me, it does not matter, I leave immediately, just enough time to put something in the suitcase and call work. My boss reassures me and hopes that everything goes well, I can leave without problems and not think about work now, indeed he recommends me to inform him of everything. I arrive in Reggio at 11 pm, it makes no sense to continue, it would be appropriate to go to a hotel, and leave the following morning very early. I also book the ferry. I keep calling and texting Amina. I am careful not to send messages in which I reveal that I am worried, I know well that if someone read them instead of Amina, I could embarrass her or even put her in a bad situation. I write her messages like, why didn't you call me? How are you? Did you have fun in your country? Such banalities. The next morning anguished and tired, I leave. As soon as I land in Sicily, I rush to Palermo and go directly to his brother's house. Parking nearby, I arrive at his entrance door, I would have a great desire to break through the door without ringing the intercom of the ramshackle building in which he lives. The neighbors notice me almost immediately, in a working-class neighborhood like this, nothing escapes their attention. No one answers, I ring the intercom again and while I wait, a woman, an African woman, looks out of a window. She asks me who I'm looking for, I tell her that I am looking for Adel's family, I add that I am a friend of his sister. The woman does not add anything else, first she looks around to see if someone is listening to snoop, and then, in a low voice, she asks me to go up a moment in her house; she is on the second floor, interior 2. Adel's apartment is on the third floor, interior 2. The African woman opens the door for me, and I go up quickly; logically I go directly to the third floor and ring the doorbell of Adel's house. No one answers, I knock with my fists on the door, and I call Adel aloud.

After a while, I hear whispers behind the doors next to Adel's, but from his apartment nothing, only silence. Until the woman who opened the door, reaches me and invites me to enter her house. I follow her; I am desperate. Evidently, I have an agitated face; the kind woman does everything to calm me down and to put me at ease. She explains to me that here everyone does their own business, but she, seeing me desperate and alone, decided to help me as much as she can. Without wasting time thanking her for her courtesy, I ask about Adel's family. She replies that Amina, Adel's sister, came from Florence about ten days ago, and that they both left. It seemed strange to her that Adel left his wife and children alone here in Italy. A couple of days ago, the other brother came, the one who works in France, and together with Adel's wife and children, they left with many luggage, but she does not know for where. However, she adds, they put so much stuff in their luggage, that they emptied their little house. Anyway, now the house is uninhabited, she can confirm it because, living right under them, she no longer hears the many noises coming from their apartment, continuous noises both day and night. I don't know what to think! While the kind woman puts the water to heat to prepare a tea, I explain to her that I came to take Amina, who was supposed to return yesterday by plane from her country with her brother. The woman is a bit interdicted; I think she sensed something, but she does not go further. She just tells me that, according to her, they have been leaving for a long time; so many luggage indicates that they will not return for a long time. I ask her, "What about Adel's work? He will have to go back to work!" she replies, "Which job! He had odd jobs, he was able to bring home just the necessary to live, and he did not have a secure job and not even a continuous job". Everything is clear to me; they all went to their country and maybe they will never come back. I ask the woman if it was possible that they forced Amina to stay with them in their country, Amina has a job and a residence permit in Italy! Maybe they forced her to stay there, breaking the law! The woman is frightened and explains to me that she does not know these things; she claims that she is now busy. I've just had a few sips of tea when I realize I'm no longer welcome. I get up to leave, I thank her and as I am about to leave the woman takes me by the arm and looking me straight in my eyes, she says, "Believe me, I would like to help you, but I myself am just an immigrant without a residence permit. My husband is busy working for our three children all day and I go to clean people's homes for little money. We cannot afford to expose ourselves, especially since my husband will soon be regularized by his employer, who has clearly warned that he does not want problems of any kind". I reassure her, "Don't worry, I understand. You have already been too kind to invite me into your apartment and above all to open the door and allowed me to personally check that no one lives in Adel's apartment". I get out quickly and go back to the car, so I decide to go to the police; I have no choice but to hope for their help. I arrive at the police station. I explain to the guard at the entrance that a foreign friend of mine with a residence permit has not given her news for four days. The guard at the entrance is reluctant to let me through, perhaps he believes that I am a rash person, but, convinced by my insistence, he makes me sit in a waiting room. I wait for about an hour, and then finally another police officer takes me to his office, where another person also works. I tell the story trying to be as clear as possible, and hiding, for the moment, the nature of the relationship between Amina and me. The police officer explains to me that the girl is of age and that she has not left without giving an explanation. They are not allowed to investigate whether the girl herself has decided to stay in her country or to extend her visit to family members. Finally, he adds that I am not even a family member of her. True, I am no one to the law; I am just a desperate woman who cannot declare her love for her woman. My hands are tied, and I am helpless. The police officer adds that there must be valid reasons before activating the 'extraordinary commissioner for missing persons'. He asks me if the girl is unable to understand and take an action, if she has suffered trauma, if she has been mistreated. I answer that she is mentally healthy, that she has not been mistreated, but I add that the family, indeed her brother, did not want her to move to Florence. Finally, I decide, I realize that I am not helping to motivate any investigations, so I decide to spill the beans and tell everything. In the meantime, the commissioner is also added, who is in time to listen to the whole story. As I narrate my relationship with Amina, it is as if I am exposed naked, stripped of my privacy in front of the eyes of these men. Fortunately, they are very understanding and kind, indeed they don't pay attention to the lesbian part of my story, as if it were a habitual relationship for them. Well, I think, now I feel really understood and comfortable. The inspector asks me for Adel's address, then tells me they will contact the airline to find out if Amina has boarded. In the end, they advise me to go home and relax. Before leaving, I confirm that I prefer to stay in Palermo, to be at their disposal for everything. When I get out of the police station, I'm more confident, as if this bad story is going to have a good ending. I decide to find a hotel not far from the police district and settle there. I phone my boss to update him, and then answer my friends who have been bombarding me with phone calls all morning. I couldn't answer earlier because I had turned down the ringer on my cell phone, but I kept checking it out hoping to see a message or a call from Amina. After lunch, I decide to take another tour around Adel's house. I hope not to meet the kind woman who opened me earlier; I don't want to disturb her further. I ring Adel's doorbell, I wait again, I ring again, but nothing; I go back to the hotel waiting for news. The next day I am still anxiously waiting, around noon the inspector calls me asking me to go to them for the latest news. I hurry. The inspector understands my anguish and does everything to calm me down; he offers me a fizzy drink. He tells me that they got in touch with the airline and that Ms. Amina's return ticket was canceled the day after she arrived in her Country. I have a start, "But how canceled! It certainly wasn't she who did it. Someone has canceled it so that she will not come back. I'm sure. Amina didn't tell me she canceled the return ticket, so someone did it without her knowing. She is now a prisoner there by them. Do something. Activate the embassy". The police commissioner tries to calm me down, "Madam, this is a long and difficult procedure, indeed Ms. Amina being of age and also having problems at work, as you reported, she will have decided to stay in her Country, and perhaps she does not have the courage to tell you that she wants to stay with her family! She probably has trouble explaining to you that she doesn't want to go back to Italy! She may have followed her parents' advice!" I snap and reply nervously, "It's impossible, you have to believe me, we love each other, we are a couple, and we are a family. She went to her country just to see her sister who had just married". The police officer still begs me to calm down. Then he tells, "Madam, we are tracking down the owner of Adel's house to get detailed news, and he goes on to assure me that Adel's personal data will be processed for an eventual international notification. However, in order to proceed with international service there must be a crime, at least a presumable crime. Ms. Amina has never asked for assistance from the police in Italy and has never communicated to the social centers her discomfort because of her brother. Finally, I assure you that I will evaluate with the prefecture the involvement of the 'police for international cooperation': Interpol. However, before activating this procedure, we must examine and evaluate all the elements in our possession, and now we only have your statements. I can confirm that as soon as possible we will proceed with the interrogation of the owner of the rented apartment, or simply used by Mr. Adel and his family". Sara is also advised to return to Florence, they will keep her constantly updated on any developments. Sara insists on staying in Palermo, even if only to go to Adel's apartment other times, in case any of them return. The commissioner repeats that it is useless; they will get in touch with the owner for the registry searches of Adel and family. This time Sara leaves the police station discouraged. She understands that she has no hope, it is clear to her that she must submit to a necessary slowness of bureaucracy, especially since the presence of a crime is not evident. She decides to stay one more day in Palermo, during which she goes several times to Adel's apartment hoping that someone will answer. However, nothing, she always finds emptiness and silence, an emptiness and a silence that torment her. She suffers more than ever from the lack of Amina; she imagines her perhaps alive, indeed certainly alive, but certainly mistreated and held captive.

Amina forever.

As soon as she returns home to Florence, Sara finds the warmth and company of her friends and her boss, indeed he begs her to keep him informed of developments. Her boss tells that in case the police fail to resolve this situation, he could talk to some of his friends who have acquaintances with embassies on the other side of the Mediterranean, but he does not specify anything else. Meanwhile Sara continues to write messages on Amina's mobile phone, very serene messages so as not to show that in Italy everyone is on alert, as the polis commissioner also advised her. A couple of days after her return home, she decides to write undaunted to Amina, although in vain now, "Have you met Anbar's husband? I'm curious to know what he's like!" This time with great surprise, as soon as the message is sent, she sees that it has been received and someone is reading it. Her heart leaps down her throat, hope returns, she is happy, she rejoices. She waits anxiously for the answer; the mobile phone shows that someone is composing a message on the other side. She waits and waits, but nothing, from time to time she sees that someone composes a message, but then stops. Sara returns to her affliction, she understands that those who are writing certainly do not do it on impulse, indeed it seems to be looking for the most suitable words. Finally, a message arrives,

"Hi Sara, don't worry about me, I'm fine, and I couldn't reply to your messages because the phone was broken, but now I changed it and recovered the card. Please be calm, I will notify you when I plan the return trip". Sara does not believe a word of the message. She thinks about it a bit and then decides to set a trap. She doesn't know how, she thinks a little more, until she remembers that Amina when she comes home, always whistles that tune, the same tune of a few notes. Then she immediately writes, "Hi Amina, thank goodness that you answer me, I was worried about you, despite knowing that you are in good hands at your family's house. The neighbor asked me about you because he no longer hears the tune that you always whistle when you hang out your clothes on the balcony, at the back of the house. He asked me if you were gone!" Amina and Sara generally, if they do not use the dryer, hang the clothes to dry in the attic where there are shared drying racks for apartment block. She sees that someone reads it and then starts writing something. This time the answer comes quickly, "Sara, didn't you tell the neighbor that I left to visit my family? Tell him that he will listen to this tune again when I come back and hang out my clothes again on the back balcony. Now I greet you because I am busy, I write to you when I can. Bye". Now Sara knows for sure that it wasn't Amina who wrote, or even if it was Amina, she wanted to send the wrong message to make it clear that someone controlled her. She would like to write again, but she does not, she is afraid of exaggerating and making the interlocutors suspicious. Instead, she immediately telephones the police commissioner in Palermo and informs him of these last messages. The police commissioner is now less hesitant, assures her that he will also add this element in the documentation, and asks Sara to send him a copy of these messages. Finally, the commissioner informs Sara that they have spoken to the owner of the house, who asserts that the house was given to Adel on probation. Since it had been "probated" for years, the police proceeded to fine the owner for failure to notify the police headquarters of tenants in his apartment. The owner of the house must also remain available for a possible inspection in the apartment. However, the owner is exonerated from any involvement, apart from the fines he will have to pay for his bureaucratic shortcomings. Indeed, he has nothing to do with the alleged kidnapping.

That evening Sara rummages in the drawer of memories, finding, among many others, a poem that Amina wrote to her, one longer than usual:

"Cloud, cloud fleeing far away on the horizon,

You are woven with a thread of strength; your bonds are courage.

The wind that pushes you far away is not an enemy, nor is the sea that you look at from above an enemy.

I watch you from the shore as you disappear more and more.

You leave me and I entrust my love to you, take it far where everything is shiny.

Travel well with this load of affection.

I will never see you again, cloud woven of strength, but wherever you land, remember me.'

She is moved and decides to carry this poem always with her, as an indivisible bond between her and Amina.

After that one message from someone who used Amina's cell phone, Sara doesn't receive any more. She does not wait any longer; she decides to take a period of vacation at work. Her boss does not rush her; on the contrary, they meet several times and talk for a long time about how to contact Amina again. He has a dear childhood friend, a person who has a prominent position in an Italian embassy on the other side of the Mediterranean. Having examined the situation and the long bureaucracy, Sara considers that she must do it herself, and not wait for the police, who unfortunately still do not have enough elements to be able to consult Interpol. From Amina still no news. However, the last few months did not pass unnecessarily; Sara has not stopped a single day to organize the trip to go and pick up her woman, her love. She is convinced, no one will be able to stop her, and she is determined to go directly to the home of Amina's parents, even if it may be too risky. She does not give up; she plans a detailed plan to free her. Unexpectedly, a friend of theirs comes to her aid; he is Cris. He knows the language of that country, being the mother originally from a Country bordering that of Amina; then he offers to accompany her. Sara wants to organize everything down to the smallest detail: initially she plans to leave camouflaged as a man to be freer to move. Later she is forced to desist because it implies having to procure false documents, and if she is discovered, she could be arrested. The days go by and from Amina still no message. Sara continues to write, but now she is convinced that if Amina were alive, she would surely be held captive. All their friends collaborate to devise a plan that can be achieved with few risks; it seems they decide that Sara faces this journey with Cristian and Cris. Cristian does not want Cris to leave alone; he fears that he will get into trouble. Finally, they decide that Sara and Cris will pretend to be husband and wife, while Cristian could travel alone, on his own, without showing any connection with the two fake spouses. As soon as they arrive at their destination, Cris could investigate by wandering around the house of Amina's parents. Sara hopes, in this way, to be able to contact first Alif, Amina's cousin, and then hope that the boy is on their side. Now they have no alternative. Anbar is also very fond of Amina; they could try to contact her too! In short, they have to get in touch with someone from the family, but Cris will do it, since he speaks the local language, while Sara in this first phase will remain on the sidelines in the shadows. In the event that the first contact with Alif or Anbar is successful, they can find out what happened to Amina. They will know if Amina wants to stay of her own free will in her Country for some reason unknown to everyone. This would be a very unlikely scenario, but in that case, Sara will be able to confront Amina and they will be able to clarify each other. The second scenario, the almost certain one, is that Amina is held captive. In this case, they imagine that it would be useless to try to free her by having the local police intervene, nor could the police commissioner from Italy help. However, they cannot organize a precise and detailed plan to bring her back to Italy. After a few more days, during which everyone has run aground and does not know how to solve the situation, Sara has an intuition: they will return with Amina, as refugees on a boat, at least she and Amina will return like this, or maybe just Amina. They will embark her on a boat of refugees, and as she will arrive in Italy, someone will go to pick her up. Meanwhile, the two Cris and Sara will move quickly by train in the neighboring Country of Amina and from there they will take the first flight to Italy. Everyone applauds this plan, the last details will be defined later, and they are determined to stay there as long as it takes to contact Amina. Sara's boss, making the decisive move, reports that he spoke with a childhood friend of his who works at the embassy of a Country bordering that of Amina. This embassy official has contacts of smugglers who are believed to be reliable. In the embassy, they help fight illegal immigration, so this official knows a little bit about everyone. However, they cannot go to his office, but will have to meet him in a third Country, one different from Amina's and the one where the official's embassy is. For heaven's sake, this official would not do anything illegal, but he absolutely does not want to leave a trace of his meeting with Sara and her accomplices. Everything begins to be defined, preparations are in full swing. They carry with them a large sum of cash; surely, they will have to pay someone in cash, in euros, without a trace. Sara does not want to spend any more time, she is convinced that Amina is suffering, and she is determined to stop this torture as soon as possible. Finally, they decide to leave during the month of May to have the advantage, when they cross the Mediterranean by boat with other refugees, to have good weather and that it will not be cold. On the day of departure Cristian still remains in Florence, as scheduled Sara and Cris arrive at their destination first and only the following day Cristian also joins them, staying in a different hotel. Everything seems to be going well: Sara and Cris avoid showing them off, indeed Sara wears local clothes to disguise herself and when they are in a public place, Cris tries always to speak in the local language. Already the day after their arrival, the two pass for the first time in front of Amina's house, leaving a taxi not far away, and then continue walking. Sara is well disguised and unrecognizable. They also pass in front of Alif's house, hoping to run into him, but unfortunately, they do not meet him. Amina left her parents' house after the wedding, but they hope to meet her anyway. When they return to the hotel, they pretend not to know Cristian, approach him as if it were a casual encounter, and exchange information secretly, just like spies in certain movies. They decide that Cristian will go to meet the embassy official, while the other two will be busy patrolling the area of Amina and Alif's house. Cristian, therefore, is absent for a couple of days to contact the official. Sara and Cris, always changing clothes, pass several times in front of the house of Amina and Alif, sometimes walking sometimes in a taxi. Until one day Sara sees Alif, she immediately makes Cris understand with a predefined nod. Cris orders the taxi driver to stop a little further on and the two get out of the car without haste. Always walking calmly, they make sure to come across Alif. As soon as they arrive in front of him, Cris, speaking the local language, asks him for the way to the museum of contemporary art. Alif is stunned and asks why they came here if the museum is so far away? Cris, with a serious look, replies that there is a person who would like to talk to him. Alif is surprised, he is not sure he understands, so he asks him to explain better. Cris tells him, in a persuasive voice, to stay calm because he has to give him a message from Sara, the Italian lady. Meanwhile Sara remains well covered and does not show herself. Alif shuts up, he doesn't move, he looks around briefly to make sure no one observes him. Cris continues in a low voice and smiling as if he were asking him for information, "Let's get away for a moment, and I'll tell you Sara's message". Alif does not trust him, he thinks that someone wants to hurt him, and he tries to get away. At this point Sara enters the scene, "Alif stop I'm Sara, please help me, I'm desperate". Alif stops immediately surprised, for a few seconds he does not know what to say or do. He is confused; he still looks around and beckons the two to follow him in silence. Without adding anything else, he starts in the opposite direction to his home. The two follow him at a distance, discreetly, understand or hope that Alif wants to take them to a secluded area, where he is not known, perhaps to be able to talk to them without any witnesses. After about a couple of kilometers, as soon as they have arrived in a dirt and uninhabited area, with tall and sparse bushes, Alif stops and waits for the two to reach him. Alif: "Are you crazy! What did you come here for?" Sara: "Why are we crazy? We have no more news of Amina. She had to come here for about ten days to visit her newly married sister, and after about three months, we don't know what happened to her". Alif seems to have an intuition to break free and finish this story right now: "Didn't they tell you that Amina is dead? Didn't you know? Didn't Adel inform you?" Cris is shocked, Sara feels herself sinking, but she too has her intuition, perhaps more cunning than Alif's, "How did she die? Don't tell lies, I spoke to Amina a week ago!" Alif can't pretend to be surprised, he falls into the trap, "How is it possible! How did Amina manage to escape her husband's control and call you?" Sara is devastated, she has just found out that Amina has married, but at least she knows that she is alive. She does not show her feelings, remains apparently frosty, and continues to make her surprise moves to anticipate Alif, "Dear Alif, Amina only had time to tell me that she married against her will and asked me to come here to greet her for the last time". Alif fell into the trap. He doesn't even imagine that Sara is making up everything at the moment, and so far, she's been really good. Alif, "I don't know what Amina told you, but you can't see her, it's not possible. Go away and go back to your country, I will think about reporting this meeting to Amina, and then, I don't think Amina really wants to meet you". Sara does not give up, "No Alif, we will not leave if we do not say goodbye to Amina. At least until we see her for the last time we won't leave". Cris finally enters the conversation, "Alif, we absolutely will not leave if we do not first meet Amina for the last time. We are determined to stay here all the time we need and, if necessary, we also go to the police". Alif begins to be afraid; he no longer responds. In reality, all three of them shut up for a few minutes, waiting for Alif to give in. The boy can't break free, and hesitantly replies, "Okay. I do not know how I will do it; I do not know how I will have to organize, but I will try to make you talk to Amina ... I don't know if I have to involve Adel! ... It would be better if you only talk to Amina by phone, is that okay with you?" Sara without wasting time evaluates that it is better to contact Amina at least by phone rather than risk not hearing her or seeing her ever again. Then she replies, "Of course Alif, by phone it would be fine. Give me her number and I'll talk to her", "No - adds Alif immediately - she does not have a phone, they do not leave her with a phone, and she is segregated at home. I could call her husband, and with an excuse ask him to pass me Amina. Conversely, I call when the husband is not at home hoping that her mother-in-law will pass her to me, but I have to come up with a good excuse to make me talk to Amina directly without making her guardians suspicious. Yes, because she lives in her husband's house with her mother-in-law, father-in-law and two sisters-in-law who are still unmarried". "Well, replies Sara confident, get some ideas in your mind and call her now. Now it's morning and her husband will definitely be at work". Alif is fed up with this pressure and so much tension. He thinks and focuses on what to do or how to do it. They remain a few more minutes in silence. Meanwhile, Sara mentally organizes a short speech for Amina to tell her, quickly, that she does not leave without her, whatever it costs. Luckily, Alif doesn't speak Italian, so she can talk to Amina freely. Finally, Alif finds a good excuse, while hesitating; he dials the house number of Amina's husband. The phone rings, and rings, then a woman's voice answers, Sara does not recognize to be Amina's. They speak in their own language and not even Cris understands what they say, as they speak in a local dialect. After the conversation with the woman, Alif waits for someone else to come to the phone, then a woman's voice greets Alif, Sara finally recognizes Amina's voice on the other side of the communication. Alif explains the situation to her, and on the other side, Amina is silent. Then Alif adds something more and finally Amina answers, then the boy passes the phone to Sara, who is very happy, finally it's done, "Amina I'm Sara, I came here with friends to take you home to Italy. I'm not leaving until you come with us". Amina cannot answer in Italian so as not to be discovered by someone who is evidently next to her in the house, she is forced to say something in the local language, and then add in a low voice: "Yes", and then immediately repeats in a low voice "Yes, yes". After that, she resumes speaking in the local language. Sara understood that with those 'yeses', pronounced in Italian, Amina made it clear that she wants to be saved. At this point Sara quickly tells her to be ready because she does not yet know how, but she will be able to know where she lives and somehow reach her. Alif senses that Sara is saying something dangerous and picks up the phone from her hand. Sara does not give in, and tries a slight defense, but then leaves the phone almost immediately, does not want to irritate Alif, their only contact with Amina. The boy feels relieved by the commitment, imagines that he has done his duty and wants to leave, "Are you satisfied? Now you can go back to your Country". Sara stops him holding him by the arm, and in an authoritarian attitude says to him, "I don't understand why we can't go and visit Amina's mother and Sister Anbar whom I know well! I want to wish her all the best for the wedding!" and Alif, "Are you crazy? I can't, you don't understand that Amina is segregated and both she and her family cannot have any contact with her friends in Italy!". Sara does not let him go, holding the sleeve of his shirt clutched in her hand, adds desperately, "Alif, we all know that Amina is segregated and that she cannot go out or talk to anyone. However, does all this seem right to you? I know you love your cousin very much! You two were very fond, so why do you allow all this? I want to meet Amina at least once. It's true that she got married, but that has nothing to do with wanting to meet her for the last time". Alif replies that he can't do anything about it, that here the rules are these, that parents choose husbands over daughters. He himself is in danger, if they discovered all this he would be punished too. He adds that the sons are also subject to the will of their parents. Nevertheless, Sara insists and even Cris, speaking in the local language, tries to convince him. Finally, Alif has no alternative; yields to their demands. He wants to think better about how to organize this meeting, so he will show up as soon as he makes a decision. Sara gives to him her phone number and Cris's, managing to get from Alif the promise that he would definitely call. The group breaks up and the two return to their hotel, where they find Cristian who has good news. Cristian reports the meeting he had with the embassy official; he managed to get the name of a smuggler, a safe person who does not play tricks, and above all is not a delinquent. Well, Sara thinks, it seems that things are really going well. They spend a couple of days waiting for a phone call from Alif, useful days to organize the escape. Cris calls the smuggler and learns that he only organizes a weekly trip to Italy. The cost of his travel is high; it is 3500 euros per person because he guarantees a certain security. The smuggler explains that the journey is safe because the migrant is not abandoned in case of danger; they also provide a life jacket and a GPS tracker. It is necessary to meet with him the week before departure and pay everything in advance. This could be a complication because it is a bit difficult to communicate their availability to the smuggler a week before departure. The problem is that, having to pick up Amina and having to run away quickly, they cannot calculate the exact day a week before. Nevertheless, the important thing is to have made this contact and above all to have known the price in order to collect the necessary money. Not knowing who will leave with Amina, they decide to collect 11,000 euros, which is the sum necessary for the trip of two women and a man, plus extras. They borrow them from friends from Italy, who send them in various ways immediately. The initial plan was that Cristian and Sara would leave with Amina, while Cris, knowing the local language, would go by train to a neighboring Country without leaving a trace of his movement, and from there take a plane back to Italy. Then Cristian adds that the smuggler told him about the possibility of remaining hidden near boarding for a few days, but this will cost 50 euros per day per person. All three of them suspect that this stay will be dangerous; they will be at the mercy of unforeseen events. The smuggler ensures the trips, but the stay on site before the trip depends on various factors, not on him. They could be caught by the police or assaulted by a rival gang. Considering all this, they change their mind and decide that Cris will leave with the two women, since, if they find themselves in dangerous situations during the days of waiting, at least Cris speaking the local language can be more helpful. Finally on the third day comes Alif's phone call. They make an appointment in the same place where they had left off three days earlier. This time all three go to the appointment with Alif. As soon as they arrive, Alif is upset when he sees them arriving with a third person, but Sara reassures him and reminds him that she has come with many friends and that she will leave only if she can talk to Amina personally. She adds that there are two other friends in the hotel waiting for instructions. Alif confesses that he suffered a lot when they forced Amina not to return to Italy and later to marry against her will. Now Sara knows for sure that Amina's husband raped her. Listening to Alif's words, Sara feels a strong grudge and a desire for revenge. For a moment, she is determined to buy a butcher's knife, enter the house of Amina's husband, make a massacre, and run away with her beloved. However, it is only a wish that cannot be realized. Alif reports that generally, Amina is never alone, one of the two unmarried sisters-in-law is always at home, and that she absolutely cannot go out. Then he lays out his plan: the only solution is that he goes to visit Amina, when she is alone with one of the sisters-in-law, and while he distracts the sister-in-law, Amina can sneak out on the balcony, which is on the mezzanine floor, and talk a few minutes with Sara. Only Sara will be able to come with him, and she will have to wear local clothes to go unnoticed. Sara approves the plan, so Alif before leaving, warns them that the right time will be in four days: generally, on Thursdays the women of the house go to the market and leave Amina alone with one of the two sisters-in-law. Finally, now they can organize the plan. Sara decides that as soon as Amina goes out on the balcony, she will help her climb over it, and both will leave immediately. In the meantime, they will have to rent a car with Cristian driving. Cris, on the other hand, will have to stay near the balcony like any passer-by, to check what happens after Amina's escape. Afterwards they will all meet directly in an established place, near the one where the smuggler stays the people before departure. The morning they go to the balcony and pick up Amina, they will have to pay the hotel bill and leave their suitcases in the rented car. After the kidnapping, Cristian will accompany the two women to the established place, where they will wait for Cris to join them. Then everyone will go to the smuggler. Finally, Cristian will bring the car back to the owner, take the first train to the neighboring State, from where he will finally get on the first plane to Italy. It seems that everything can work, but no one knows if there will be variables. While they wait with fibrillation for the appointed day, Cris meets the smuggler and pays him; the first trip available is unfortunately for Sunday, so they will have to stay at least three nights at the smuggler. Not bad, the important thing is that they found a place to leave on Sunday. Sara dyes her hair black and tries to curl them with a curling iron that she had previously brought with her. It seems that everything is ready. Cristian and Cris, however, only now realize that they are taking big risks, and above all Cristian begins to have doubts and fear. He is afraid he will not be able to cross the border to go to the neighboring State, for which both Cris and Cristian have already previously applied for an entry visa. Because of these doubts, they decide that Cris will return by plane, while Cristian will go with the smugglers; overall, at least there is Amina who speaks the local language just in case. Meanwhile, they hide some extra money, well sewn into the folds of the pants; Sara wears men's clothes to be more agile and avoid being noticed. Cris books via internet the plane trip from the neighboring Country to France, unfortunately for that day there is no flight available to Italy. Not bad, the important thing is that he manages to reach the European Union.

As promised, on Thursday morning they receive Alif's phone call. The boy warns them that they must be in the usual place, in about an hour. Damn they have little time, Cris rushes to rent the car, while Sara and Cristian prepare the few luggage, just three backpacks, indeed they had got rid of the superfluous the day before throwing everything in the garbage cans. Finally, Cris arrives a little late; as a result, they arrive 45 minutes late for the appointment with Alif. The man gets angry and wants to blow everything up, but they convince him to continue. Finally, all four leave for the house of Amina's husband. As soon as they arrive near the apartment, Alif orders the two men to leave or wait far, far away, while Sara stays with him. Sara is excited and scared at the same time. She is going to meet Amina after a long time, and then they have to run away, and all the other worries... She lacks breath and is about to faint, but she gains strength, goes on without showing any fear. Arrived in front of the building, there are few people on the street, and Alif confirms that he has already spoken with Amina, so everything is organized well. Sara stays near the balcony dressed in local clothes and with her head covered, she also has a shopping bag with vegetables inside, as if she were a woman who has just gone to the nearby market. She waits and waits more and more in tension, finally the balcony opens, and a figure comes out that looks like Amina, she too is covered and it is only possible to see the eyes. Yes, it's her. Amina as soon as she sees Sara does not waste time, with an agile leap she overcomes the railing and lands effortlessly on the dusty road. The two women without even saying goodbye head calmly towards the waiting car; it is not the case to waste time in greetings. Cris who has lurked nearby observe the scene. Sara and Amina, holding tight, head towards the car. They enter without haste and Cristian leaves calmly, slowly so as not to arouse suspicion. They travel at low speed, until they arrive almost outside the city, towards the agreed meeting point. During the journey by car, the two women hold hands strongly, both cry. Then finally, stop and call their accomplice remained on the spot. Cris immediately replies and reports that they have only recently noticed the escape. He saw Alif looking out onto the balcony and being stunned when he found it empty. Then he approached the house and could hear that Alif was arguing with the girl asking her not to overact in front of everyone, she could not make a scandal, her family would have paid the consequences. At this point, after the phone call with Cris, Amina decides to make her move: before leaving, she stole her sister-in-law's phone, and with that, she calls home. Her sister-in-law replies and Amina explains that she has gone away taking advantage of Alif's visit, that she is now wandering around the city alone and that she will return home only if they guarantee that she can lead a normal life. Then she adds that she will still go to a safe place and stay there until her husband and father-in-law decide to accept her conditions. She will spend the night at the home of an old school friend of hers. Finally, she explains that Alif knew nothing about her escape, because she decided to run away suddenly, without premeditation. In this way, Amina was so witty and good that she made sure to postpone at least 48 hours, the search for her by family members. Also, in this way, his family members do not alert the police, so they will have a good margin to hide their traces and above all a good margin for Cris to leave the Country. They then call Cris again and explain that they supposedly have forty-eight hours of calm. Now he can take a taxi to reach them in the suburbs where they are waiting for him, at the established point. After about an hour Cris arrives on foot, having left the taxi a little earlier to leave no trace. At this point, they indulge in hugs even with Cris. After happily meeting, they head towards the locality of the smugglers, with so many uncertainties; however, having paid for the very expensive trip, they also bought the "security" in addition to transport. After another two kilometers, they arrive near the smuggler. Everyone heads to what looks like a mechanical workshop. Only Cris enters, he must explain to the smuggler that he will not leave but a friend of his in his place. Better, that he explains it in the local language. When Cris comes back out, he smiles, for the first time since that morning. He reports that they must leave their mobile phones and that they must have only a small luggage. Everyone leaves their cell phone to Cris who will throw them far, far away. Amina, however, first calls her sister-in-law, the girl responds crying; she is responsible for the escape, because she has not been able to guard Amina and knows well that when her mother and father return, she will be punished. Amina repeats to her that throughout the day and the following day, she will not call back, may be her father-in-law and husband, as Amina says, need a long time to give in, and allow her to have a normal life. She will call her back in two days at 18.00 to know the answer of the two men of the house. The sister-in-law nods and not stopping to frown asks Amina to return, please, that if she does not return, they will blame her and beat her, other than freedom to go out. At this point Alif takes the phone from the girl's hands and orders Amina to return, but Amina replies not to worry, that she will return in a couple of days and that he will not be responsible since she will never tell anyone that it was Alif who helped her. Alif calms down, understands that his reputation towards family members depends on Amina, if Amina does not tell the truth; he will not be accused and punished. Indeed, Amina makes him understand that he is blackmailed.

Cris and Cristian embrace warmly; they know that they will meet again directly in Italy, if everything goes according to their plans. Until now neither of them has had the courage to confess that they have many doubts, the fear that the hull could sink or suffer any accident. Cris reassures everyone by stating that the smuggler promised that the trip would be safe, for the reason that he paid more than usual. Finally, he goes away on foot to look for a taxi. They see as he walks away until small on the horizon, turns around and greets them by raising his arms. They are dejected; will they all see each other together? Cristian suffers a lot from this separation, but he is also very unscrupulous, so he bravely faces the near future. With their heads down, they head towards the mechanical workshop not far away. The smuggler as soon as he sees them, without saying anything, passes them to one of his subordinates, who, before taking them to their accommodation, searches them, yes, he also searches the women. When Cristian's turn comes, they realize that he is not from this place, that he is a European. They ask him something in their idiom but Cristian can't understand. Then the smuggler approaches and pulls him, but Amina intervenes screaming at him. The smuggler calms down, asks for something, Amina initially remains firm, then at the insistence of the smuggler, takes another 500 extra euros and delivers them to him. Only now, they are taken to their accommodation. As soon as they enter, they feel an indescribable stench of sweat and latrine. The large room is full of people lying or sitting on the ground. They are other refugees, crowded for lack of space. Amina, following the man's orders, explains that they must sit in a free corner, that the latrine is behind that ramshackle door and that they will have fish and bread as dinner, with bottled water. Bottled water is only allowed to those who have paid more. Then she explains that they will always have to stay still in their place, they can't move, they can just stand up to stretch a little, or they can go to the bathroom, nothing else. Someone will come to make further arrangements when necessary. Now all they have to do is crouch on the ground. While Amina and Sara remain embraced, Cristian is sitting attached to them. So huddled, they arrive in the evening. Shortly after sunset two men enter two henchmen of the smuggler who begin to distribute food. When they get to the three, one of them makes a comment looking at Cristian, who stupidly while taking his food ration gets up and thank them in English. The two men are surprised and exchange a few words each other smiling. Amina gets impatient, afraid, turned towards her friend, in a low voice: "Cristian, who told you to get up and discover yourself! You couldn't shut up and stand still!" and Cristian: "Sorry I saw that they smiled at me and that they were kind, I wanted to reciprocate by thanking them". Amina doesn't respond, but they realized they had exposed themselves too much. The night passes quickly. The events of that day made them fall into a deep sleep until the next morning. Early in the morning, almost everyone stands up to stretch. There is a line to use the latrine. It is a terrible situation, but everyone remains silent; from the outside, it must not hear a pin drop. They notice that there are no children or babies among the refugees. Finally, after about an hour it is Sara and Amina's turn for the latrine. First Amina enters, and when she leaves, she tells Sara that there is also a fountain to be able to wash herself clumsily, and then Sara enters. After her there are two other people and then Cristian's turn comes, he is also in line. The two women return to sit on the floor waiting for Cristian, who in the meantime has managed to enter the bathroom. While they are waiting, the two henchmen of the smuggler enter, they are those of the night before, they have to distribute breakfast: bread with a piece of cheese. As they pass through the crowd crouching on the ground, Cristian comes out of the latrine, he is without the kufiyah, he would like to wear it but his hair is wet. The two henchmen notice him again and talk to each other. Cristian feels observed, he is embarrassed, and so he decides to return quickly to his friends, wearing the kufiyah with care. As soon as the two men arrive to distribute breakfast to them too, they first deliver the food to the two women, then they hand it to Cristian, and while he stretches out his hands, they retract the food back, as if they no longer wanted to give it to him, to make him a joke, stupid, but a joke. The two men laugh, and even Cristian at first follows them laughing, then with a much more serious look, finally they also offer him his food and Cristian, while taking it, has a shiver running down his back. Sara and Amina witness the scene, and huddle closer to their friend.

Since they escaped Sara has noticed that Amina is absent, introverted. She justifies this mood as the consequence of the violence she suffered, for the stormy escape, and finally for this adventure with a completely uncertain ending. Amina is definitely leaving her family and her country. Sara wants to comfort her and give her courage, approaches her and caresses her gently, then asks if everything is fine. Amina does not respond. Sara understands that it is a very tense moment, she recognizes Amina's silence, she knows well that Amina is silent only for serious reasons. She is loyal and sincere; she must have valid and serious reasons to feel dejected and confused. Sara senses there is something that escapes her, so she decides to address the topic, "Amina, do not feel guilty, it is not your fault if that animal raped you, if you were forced to marry him. We will overcome this together too. You are not alone; you and I are one body. Don't worry, it's all over, everything will go back to the way it was before, you and I alone in our house and I swear you won't see those people again. In Italy, I went to the police, and there is an open and pending lawsuit on your family members. When we arrive, I accompany you to denounce all your tormentors, so at least we will be sure that they can no longer come to disturb us". However, Amina does not speak yet, on the contrary, she begins to cry. Sara embraces and consoles her. The whole conversation takes place whispering. In the end, Amina finally decides to answer, "Sara, you don't know one thing", Sara looks at her curiously, but adds nothing else, leaves her all the time to express herself without interrupting, "You don't know my biggest problem", and then again, a silence, not interrupted by Sara. Finally, Amina takes a deep breath, as if she needs all her breath to reveal something important and concludes, "There will be three of us living together, if you want, but if you don't want it, I'm ready to leave, to disappear. I don't want to bother you at all". Sara is confused, she does not understand what she says, she also missed that Amina mentioned "three" and not just the two of them ... She looks at her stunned and whispers, "Amina, after all we've done to come and free you, you tell me you're going to live elsewhere if I don't want you to be with me! Are you okay? What problem do you have?" Then suddenly Sara is silent, understands, and without adding anything else, gently slips her hand under Amina's robes and touches her belly. It is slightly swollen. Yes, it is; indeed, Amina is so thin that every slightest swelling is noticeable almost immediately. Sara is amazed. She expected everything but this. Amina insists: "If you don't want us, I disappear, I make do on my own, I'll leave". Sara does not answer; she is speechless, cold. Recovering from the shock, "What do you say, you are mine and it is not your fault what happened. We'll see what to do". Later she realizes that she has been unaffectionate, indeed quite cold, and adds, "This is our son and we will raise him, whatever it costs. He has no fault, no fault". Amina relaxes for the first time and finally Sara finds the Amina of all time. Then Sara adds, "Indeed, our son will be the purpose of our lives". Both begin to cry in silence. Cristian sleeps, he doesn't notice anything. It's Friday evening, the day before Amina said she would call her husband again to find out if he accepted her condition to return home. Probably only tomorrow or maybe the day after tomorrow her family members would worry and could understand that Amina has not simply moved away from home. They still have to spend a whole night, another day and then a whole night; maybe they manage to leave the Country before the family members go to the police. The two women are serene as they can be in this situation; both realize that they have become mothers, that they have a child, unexpected one, but precisely for this reason more loved. While the two women talk to each other, Cristian wakes up; he can't stand still curled up. He wants to go out, walk a little, but Sara and Amina stop him decisively. Cristian calms down, for the moment, he desists, but he proposes to go out a little, at least at night when everyone is asleep. The two women beg him not to make mistakes, to stay calm. Now it is important to be quiet to conclude this adventure, and then they are thinking about Cris who, according to their plan, should already have reached Europe, since the night before, at most today, which is Friday. Especially Cristian, thinking of his partner, cannot stand still in his place curled up on the ground. The second evening arrives in the shack, and after dinner of bread and fish, they manage to fall asleep. Sara makes sure to sleep in direct contact with Cristian to control him. Cristian manages to stay curled up and not move from his place. The next morning, Saturday, they wonder what Amina's family is doing! Maybe they haven't turned to the police yet, for fear of a scandal, or they're still waiting, hoping that Amina will call back home. Surely, Alif was exonerated for this escape. Well, now they have to stay good in their place and spend this last day, then the next night, maybe night, they would leave. Time passes slowly, and the discomforts become more and more annoying. However, they are accustomed to using a latrine together with about forty people, so many are crammed into that warm and sultry hut. No one bothers the other; they are all united by the same fate. Even the day of Saturday passes without any problem, until the last night comes. Amina and Sara reveal their secret to Cristian; they also do it to distract him and to pass the time. Cristian is thrilled; he claims to be the adoptive father of the child. Very happy for the news he adds that this child has two mothers and two fathers, and that Cris will be very happy for this news. Mentioning Cris, remind everyone of their friend; they become sad, they hope that everything will go well during the crossing of the Mediterranean. Sunday morning also arrives, and everyone is awake and anxious. They are not afraid; they just have a certain fear and a lot of uncertainty about what will happen. They, certain of the high amount they have spent, just to guarantee a peaceful crossing, manage in part to calm down and be confident. Their feverish wait is interrupted at lunchtime, when the two henchmen arrive to bring the usual fish with a little bread and water, always packaged only for the three of them. Oddly enough, they are served last, and when Cristian's turn comes, they beckon him to follow them out. Cristian does not move; on the contrary he clings to Sara showing as if the woman were his wife. However, they take him by the arm and try to get him up. Cristian resists, Sara tries to keep him on the ground, when one of them slaps her so hard that she bumps into Amina, who in turn starts screaming too. Then the two henchmen become more aggressive, they also hit Cristian in the head making him fall to the ground, then they take their machine guns, which they carry hanging from behind, and point them towards Amina and Sara. They say something in their language, and Amina runs towards Sara hugging her with her eyes closed in fear. The refugees present turn away from them in terror. Then they drag Cristian by the hair and arms out of the shack. Cristian continues to scream, while Amina and Sara get up and run to the door too. As soon as outside they hear Cristian's screams coming from a small shed nearby, at this point Amina screams with all the strength, she has, alarming everyone and asking for help. This confusion attracts the attention of other smugglers who rush to tell the woman to shut up, but Amina explains what happens and points to the small shed, from where in the meantime Cristian continues to scream in despair. The men, who have rushed, go to the shed and come out with the two henchmen held by the hair, and take them away kicking them. Later Cristian also comes out held up by another person who helps him to return to the two women. Cristian is battered and has his clothes partly torn. Sara, terrified, asks him how he is and he replies that fortunately the help arrived in time, and that he defended himself with all his strength. However, he has a strong pain in his ribs so much, so that he cannot stand; he has received a kick in the ribs. Everyone returns to the shack with Cristian in pain. Sara and Amina support him and bring him back to their place. They are all shocked: Sara has a bruise on her face and Cristian a probable broken rib; due to the severe pain in the side, he can hardly breathe. He lies sore all day to recover strength for the crossing. On the evening of departure, instead of the usual dinner, they distribute cheese and chocolate. Two other boys replaced the two henchmen. After dinner, they all remain silent but aware of having to leave as soon as possible. After a few interminable hours, around midnight, armed people enter the shack and choose about twenty people, including Amina, Sara and Cristian. They are all afraid; they did not expect armed people. They tell to remain completely silent and follow them without making any noise; otherwise, they will be forced to kill them. Everyone obeys, they are afraid and follow them quickly; Cristian struggles to keep up. Finally, after a couple of kilometers along the seashore, they arrive at a rubber dinghy with two large engines. Pushed by the armed men they climb into the dinghy, where they find a smuggler ready at the helm. They sit in the few free spaces, among the many crates previously loaded. Everyone receives a life jacket, and each family group a satellite phone, but the phones must be returned shortly before arrival. They are informed that they will be disembarked in about seven hours, on the coast south of Marsala. As soon as they pronounce the name of the city, Sara rejoices, and so Cristian, they already feel at home, and forget for a moment the dangers of the crossing. This trip also cost more because the illegal immigrants had asked to be disembarked directly on the coasts and not delivered to a patrol boat of the Marine Guard. Many of them intend to continue the journey beyond the Italian borders, while others, for various reasons, not least because they are jailbirds, wish to remain hidden and obtain false documents. Taking advantage of having to arrive directly on the Italian coast, the smugglers loaded the dinghy with crates with contraband goods. Disembarking directly on the coast, is also part of the plan organized by Sara, it must not turn out that Sara and her two friends have gone to pick up Amina. To organize better future complaints, Amina must figure that she managed to escape with her own strength or helped by friends of her Country. The dinghy finally leaves; they are followed at a distance by another dinghy with armed men on board. After about an hour's journey the spare dinghy goes back, leaving them alone. Only now, they can use the satellite phone they have received. Sara instantly calls Cris, who responds immediately after the first ring, he is very happy to have news, finally now he can be reassured. Sara informs him that they are heading to the south coast of Marsala and that they will arrive in about six hours. Cris confirms that he is already in southern Italy, waiting for this phone call, as agreed. He adds that with him there is also the professor, Sara's boss, with a car equipped with comforts. Then Sara would like to pass Cristian to him on the phone, but unfortunately, Cristian cannot speak, the dinghy tossed by the waves exacerbates the strong pain in his ribs, so he fears that Cris may notice that he is injured. Sara picks up the phone and explains to Cris that he is moved and can't speak. Communication must be suddenly interrupted; they see some lights in distance and all phones must be turned off. Now there must be no light on the dinghy. Sara greets Cris quickly and they hope to meet as soon as possible on the coast south of Marsala. The helmsman orders everyone to lie down so as not to see their silhouettes from afar, then the dinghy makes a sharp turn and accelerates its run. Those lights follow them and all are lying at the mercy of the waves that crash violently on the fast dinghy. Only after about two hours, those lights fade and then disappear. Someone asks what those lights were. The helmsman replies that surely it was a band of pirates. Then he explains that there are gangs looking for refugees to capture, resell or enslave them. If they had been captured, the helmsman would have ended up in the water with a gunshot in his forehead, while the refugees would have been sold as slaves and the goods stolen. The helmsman was foresighted to equip the dinghy with two powerful engines, so he managed to escape and saved his life first. Amina translates the conversation to Sara and Cristian, who are petrified by fear. No one can use the phone anymore, the helmsman takes indeed all the phones back, adds that he does it for their safety; they have been identified by other traffickers and must continue like ghosts in the middle of the sea. Now they are about halfway through the crossing, the smuggler stops the dinghy and asks to help him recharge the tanks with the tanks of gasoline he brought. He dumps the empty ones into the sea, so he too has more space to lie down. Cristian observing the scene comments, "In this way he pollutes the sea ...!", and Sara replies, "Shut up otherwise I'll punch you in the head and I'll make you shut up" and Cristian smiling, "I was joking ...", but Sara turns to him with a disapproving look. They immediately resume the fast crossing. Fortunately, the sea is calm, but the speed of the dinghy makes it jump despite its heavy load, and punctually the waves break wetting everything and everyone. Time seems to have stopped between the waves and the darkness of the sea. Fear does not abandon them; it seems that with every wave the dinghy is about to capsize. They don't even want to imagine if it sank; what would they do in the middle of the Mediterranean! They would die of hypothermia after a while or drowned or eaten by sharks. The journey seems endless, longer than they thought. While everyone is slumped and addicted to the noise of the engines and the slamming of the waves, the crossing finally comes to an end and with it the terrible fear. The dinghy arrives in sight of the Sicilian coast when it is still dark, it does not slow down, and rather it accelerates. As long as they reach a short distance from the shore, the helmsman turns off an engine and leaves only one running at low speed. Everyone sees the shore and with it their salvation. The dinghy crawls on the sand, and everyone rejoices in silence. The smuggler stops them and holding a

122

machine gun forces the passengers to unload the crates from the dinghy and take them up to a group of tall bushes near the shore. Everyone obeys orders, except Cristian who is unable to lift weights. The smuggler does not force him; others who work are there. As soon as the crates are unloaded, other men arrive and talk to the smuggler. They give him small packages and other crates, few but very heavy judging by the efforts they make to load them on the dinghy along with new tanks of gasoline. Another person joins the smuggler, he is armed with a machine gun, probably to protect a precious cargo, so they go away quickly disappearing on the horizon of the sea. All the refugees have already disappeared while the smuggler spoke with those men. Our three also left in a hurry following the refugees, but unlike them, they stop in a swampy area with tall bushes, not far from the beach. They have to proceed slowly; Cristian can't keep up with the other refugees. They don't know where to go, they have to explore the surroundings to realize where they are exactly. They remain well hidden until those men take away all the crates, about twenty, patiently loaded on their shoulders up to a couple of pick-ups not far away. As soon as they leave, the three decide to follow the footprints left by the pick-ups. There is no real road, but a sandy path, where probably a normal sedan could silt up. They realize that their friends could not come and pick them up in that area. They walk for about a kilometer until they arrive in a small cottage where is written, "Kite surf". They do not find anyone; it is still early in the morning, so they decide to follow the coast to the north, continuing on the small sandy road. They cannot venture inland in search of a paved road because of the numerous marshes that delimit cultivated fields. They are very tired, but they continue to walk for about a kilometer, until they arrive in a widening, in front of a large building, perhaps a wastewater purifier. There is a guardhouse, whose guardian can be glimpsed, Sara arranges her clothes and hair a little and decides to go and ask for information. They see her moving away towards the guardhouse, then, after a brief conversation, she returns and reports that a few hundred meters away there is a structure for bathers. She asked to use the guardian's phone, but the man, perhaps not trusting, evidently accustomed to the landings of illegal immigrants, replies that he has the company phone and that he cannot pass it to her, but that later they would surely meet someone. They get back on the road, and just outside the sight of the guardian, they decide to wash and change; in their backpacks, they brought clean clothes wrapped in plastic so as not to get them wet. In addition to washing, they relax in the cool seawater, they have walked about four kilometers, too many in the conditions in which they are. They dress up and, toned, move on. They immediately meet a jeep with a group of boys. They stop it and ask for directions; they pretend to have run out of gasoline from their car and that they have to call a friend of theirs in Marsala to be picked up. The boys fortunately provide them with a mobile phone; finally, Sara can communicate with their rescuers. Cris replies, he sensed that this unknown number could be a phone call from them. Not knowing exactly where they were, Sara passes the phone to the boys who explain to Cris how to reach them. Then the boys greet them and leave, while the three sit on the ground determined not to take a step anymore. They have communicated their position, so they wait exhausted to be reached. After about another thirty minutes the professor's off-road vehicle arrives first, the area is impervious for cars, as a result the off-road vehicle could arrive earlier. The meeting concludes all their efforts, everyone embraces the professor with joy. While they are refreshing, they can also see in the distance Cris' car trudging along the sandy path. Cris as soon as he reaches them splashes out of the car and goes to hug his partner first; they remain tight for several minutes. Cristian feels a strong pain in the rib but does not complain; he does not want to interrupt this moment. Cris assures him that this was the first and last time he left him in a dangerous situation that they were unconscious for not understanding the risk they took. Cris then embraces Sara and Amina. Amina does nothing but thank everyone. They stay there for a couple of hours telling each other about the latest events. As soon as they are refreshed, they decide to return directly to Florence, where Amina will denounce all those who have kidnapped and segregated her. She will also denounce the rape she has suffered and all that will be necessary to condemn her tormentors. During the return journey Sara and Amina, travel in the professor's comfortable off-road vehicle, while the two Cristian are alone in their car. They have so many things to say. They constantly repeat all the moments that have passed until their meeting, are very excited; they only shut up when Cristian collapses to sleep almost until after Rome.

Finally in Florence. Before separating, they make an appointment for the following day. Sara, Amina and their son return to their dear little house on the ground floor.

The new life.

The following day, in the afternoon, everyone meets, both the protagonists of the escape and all the friends who helped them, including Carlo and Mariana pregnant and about to give birth. They tell and repeat the events as they happened all the time; they repeat them without getting tired. Everyone pampers the four "heroes", as they are immediately defined. They realize that they should write a book about these events, and everyone agrees it will definitely be a best-seller. On the third day of their return, Sara and Amina still do not want to go out; they can postpone the complaint. They stay at home all day preparing for their new life as mothers. A week after their return, Sara takes courage, takes Amina by the hand and, without waiting for her consent, lays her on the bed and strips her. She begins to excite her, but Amina has lost all interest in the sex. Sara insists with determination and continues until Amina manages to get rid of her ghosts, and slowly resumes her sex life with Sara. They spend that first night in which they really feel together, finally serene and far from any danger and above all Amina tastes freedom again. The next morning both feel strong and determined to fight. Sara accompanies Amina to the police station, where the girl gives the names and addresses of her father, Brother Adel, father-in-law and husband. She kept women out of the charges. The police commissioner instructs a complaint for kidnapping, repeated and aggravated rape, enslavement, marriage with a serious defect of consent and a number of other no fewer secondary crimes. They also initiate Amina's divorce proceedings. Amina is a resident in Italy with a regular residence permit, and in addition to all the accusations that in themselves would invalidate the forced marriage, she can also ask for separation directly from an Italian judge. Just an Italian judge will be enough to annul her marriage. The days pass, and in the cause is involved the police station of Palermo with the old reports and complaints made by Sara. In short, Amina's family members if they want to avoid jail would do well to stay away from Italy. While the trial in absentia of the four defendants goes on, Sara takes Amina to the hospital, where they confirm that the pregnancy proceeds without problems and inform the mothers that it will not be a boy, as they thought, but will be a girl. As soon as Amina receives the news, she immediately decides that her name will be Sara Junior, and adds, Sara J for friends.

Despite all Sara's efforts, their life resumes with difficulty: both are shaken by what has happened, Amina can hardly overcome the rape she has suffered. They remain in Italy for a couple of months, to be present in the ongoing lawsuit, then in July they both decide to move to London, following Sara's new job. The professor made sure to extend Sara's hiring time, to give the girls a chance to get organized and take the ongoing cause to an advanced level. Although it will be necessary occasionally to return to Florence to be present at any convocations. Packed up the few goods, they close this period of their life; Amina is at the end of the sixth month of pregnancy. They decided not to bring anything from Italy, no furniture, only a few provisions. They want to start a new life by selecting memories to take with them. Luckily, Amina, after an initial period of depression, begins to overcome the shock of violence, thanks above all to the help of a psychologist. When all aspects of his captivity become evident, they realize it's even more monstrous than they thought. When her family forced Amina to marry, they knew that she was not virgin, so they had to pay dearly for this marriage, paying large sums to her future husband. From this marriage would depend that of the younger sister Anbar, and with it the honor of the whole family. On the wedding night her husband was very violent, he seemed to want to punish her. Amina, as a reaction to hurt him, told him that she has been with many men in Italy. At that point, the husband after raping her almost beat her to death, only the intervention of the father-in-law managed to stop him, and he interfered only to avoid causing a scandal, as always. Then the father-in-law turned to Amina's father asking him to annul the marriage feeling deceived by the new revelation of the girl. Amina's father was forced to give him an additional large sum of money, adding that they could do with Amina whatever they wanted, but not kick her out of the house. The husband then changed his mind, Amina was no longer considered as the wife of the male son of the house, but as an object in the hands of her husband, a slave for the humblest jobs in the house, always in the service of her in-laws, husband and two sisters-in-law. She was little more than a servant, however if a servant could be sent away, they could not send Amina away. When she became pregnant, things changed a bit: she was pregnant with the heir of the family. As a result, she continued to be a slave but no longer beaten. Once back in Italy, with the help of everyone, first of all Sara, these horrible memories are increasingly put in the background, thanks to the expectation of the birth of Sara J. The wait for the happy event fills their days during the first months of the new life in London. Here also, they have chosen an apartment on a ground floor; Sara said that she missed the evening whistle very much, that whistle that urged her to run to open the door and welcome her partner.

Finally, in October the little girl wants to know her mothers. Sara and Amina are both in the hospital, but the birth is long and troubled. Sara maintains continuous telephone contact with the two Cristian; this little girl is also theirs. After a whole day of labor, a beautiful and healthy baby girl is born, identical to Amina. Thank goodness, they were all worried that the baby could be born with problems due to the misfortunes suffered by Amina during the first months of pregnancy. A pregnancy that began in terror ends with childbirth in the heart of a loving family. Already the next day Amina can return home. Sara takes a few days off to be able to be next to her partner; unfortunately, they cannot have maternity or paternity leave like other couples. That winter of 2013-14 passes serenely; both look after Sara J. The presence of the baby girl in their lives overshadows all the bitterness and difficulties of the ongoing cause and the traumas suffered by both.

When little Sara J is just over five months old, their lives are further enlivened by another exceptional event. The end of the winter of 2014 brings a very pleasant news: finally, in March in the United Kingdom, it is possible celebrate marriages between same-sex couples. They will no longer live in the shadows as simple cohabitants. The amendment of the legislation relating to marriages now makes it possible to legalize, even in the eyes of the most skeptical, marriages between persons of the same sex. Without taking anything away from heterosexual marriages, homosexual marriages are added to these. Fortunately, Amina obtained a divorce from the Italian State, having repeatedly requested the presence of her husband in court to formalize the divorce, but since her husband could not present himself because the Italian authorities wanted him, the forced marriage abroad was invalidated. Indeed almost "formally" deleted because there was the thesis that it had never been valid. There is no longer any obstacle to their marriage. Sara and Amina prepare a big party, a liberating party, like a milestone that relegates all bitterness to the past. They invite Italian friends to their home in London for a big party that frees the two women, and thousands of couples like them, from years of life in a gray area. Suddenly they realize that, from now on, they have the "legitimacy and support" of the state. What they ignore is that they have been and will always be exposed to racism. The ceremony takes place in a specially organized room. The official of the Municipality is moved when Sara and Amina show up at the ceremony with the child. Little Sara J remained in Sara's arms throughout the ceremony, fortunately she remained quiet the whole time, Amina had breastfed her just before. Both witnesses and brides were moved from the beginning of the celebration. They stopped right at the end, so much so that Sara and Amina barely pronounced the formula of marriage, prevented by emotion. The witnesses could only be the two Cristian, convinced adoptive fathers of the little girl. The bad days of kidnapping and escape are long gone and no longer hurt anyone. After getting married, they adopt as a couple, little Sara J, who now, at the age of six months, has not only one mother, instead two parents. They are a family like any other, the end of oppression and injustice.

After the two ceremonies, their life in London resumes with renewed contentment, with Italian friends always in touch with them. The two Cristian, the fathers of little Sara J, as they call themselves, come to visit the new family at least in the summer and during the winter holidays. Always, each time they tell the difficult moments of the days of the kidnapping, and how they were unconscious but overall lucky. To the old and dear friends, new ones in London are also gradually added. Amina, after months of breastfeeding, resumes work, finds a job in another pub, run by an immigrant also originally from the other side of the Mediterranean, just like her. Between Amina and her new boss, a special friendship is created; he listens passionately to the terrible stories that Amina tells. Fortunately, the man understands and does not condemn her relationship with Sarah. The customers of the pub are mostly immigrants from the same country as the owner, or from the neighboring ones. Amina finds her people in them, even if she can't always share her private life. Many also maintain their lifestyle in London, under the condescending gaze of local legislation. Sara has also found a certain fulfillment in life with Amina, a fullness that for the moment keeps the monotonous everyday life out of their relationship. Thanks also to the presence of the child, for whom Sara feels an intense affection. During the second year in London, they receive bad news that saddens them a lot; unfortunately, the professor, her former head of Florence died of a heart attack. He was 73 years old and had recently retired. Sara organizes to attend the funeral in Florence but does not want to leave Amina alone with the little girl and the work. The last time they met the professor, it was at their wedding; without him, perhaps, they would not have been able to free Amina.

Sara almost always returns from work around 5.30 pm, first she picks up Sara J at kindergarten and then together they return home. Then, around 7.30 pm, when they hear the whistle, "e - C - - A A g - C - -", even Sara J, wavering, runs to get first to open the door, making the race with Sara. Then the three women remain together happy usually at home. When sometimes they go to a friend's

house, they never leave Sara J with a babysitter,
they always take her with them, unless they go to
a club, when they reluctantly entrust her to a
babysitter. Although motherhood completely
absorbs Sara at least for the first few years, soon
her nature peeps out again. She begins to feel
again her ancient and connatural desire to
"breathe", to "freedom". Evidently, it is no
coincidence, when at work, a colleague of her, a
woman whom Sara highly esteems, collects these
confidences. Her name is Lada; she is of Slavic
origin. In general, she has an unfeminine
appearance: few or no makeup, masculine
movements and little desire to show her shapes
in skimpy clothes. Sara is interested in her, she is
attracted to androgynous, thin and seemingly
fragile women, just like Amina, and Lada looks a
lot like Amina. Therefore, Sara has found this last
toy, so she begins to desert family evenings,
devoting her little free time more to Sara J rather
than to her wife. Amina feels this change, she is a
very sensitive woman, but she keeps going. She
constantly has a desire to have sex with her
partner, but Sara slips away most of the time; her
libido needs more people to be satisfied. Amina is
always calm and faithful; she has a loyalty that
sometimes irritates Sara because it emphasizes
her infidelity more. Lada is an employee of Sara's,
so Sara knows she maliciously gets an extra
chance. "It's wrong, she thinks, I can't take
advantage of it," but when she likes someone, she
loses her mind. She does not know what "fidelity"
means; indeed, she snubs that of Amina, and as
a joke, she sometimes calls her "The Faithful".

Amina, on the other hand, does not recover her personal life parallel to the loneliness in which Sara leaves her. When she is free from commitments, she spends all her time with Sara J, now she cares little about the scarce attention of her wife. While Sara, slowly, without realizing it, always goes a little further, for her part Lada is well disposed towards Sara. She is married to a Norwegian immigrant, but her husband does not care about her as he should, and in any case, Lada shows that she does not like the life with her husband. As she confessed to Sara, she married him only because, as soon as she arrived in London, she needed a roof where she could stay. The fruit that grows on the tree, sooner or later falls ripe to the ground; one evening Sara lingers more than usual in the office and asks Lada to stay. She alerted Amina of her delay, so one less annoyance. That evening after work, Lada enters Sara's office and finds Sara sitting watching her intensely as she enters. Sara mentions a certain job that should be completed but pretends to have headaches and not have the strength to complete it. She adds, "Lada I'm sorry if I made you stay in the office for nothing". Unexpectedly Lada replies in the best way for Sara, "No Sara, don't worry, I'm happy to stay and keep you company". Sara takes the initiative; this is the right evening. She gets up, walks in the room up behind Lada's back, looks at her from behind, she is irresistible. Despite being of Slavic origin, she is low and thin, with blond hair, almost white. Sara's curiosity does not stop there, she no longer resists, and she approaches and puts her hands on her shoulders pretending to start a relaxing massage. Lada at first pretends to be surprised, then immediately relaxes, more and more, like a vortex that attracts both, the massage becomes more and more intense. Until Lada, excited, gives a kiss on the hand that massages her. Sara, holding her gently by the chin, reciprocates the kiss with an intense one on the mouth. In a second, the two women are lying on the ground, undressing quickly with greed. They kiss, love each other and give vent to everything that until then had been relegated only to their desires. A few hours pass, then Sara, now satisfied, clearly pretends to realize that it is late. She gets up quickly, showing herself worried, goes to the bathroom to wash herself to try to erase the smell of Lada from her body. Lada remains exhausted on the ground, languidly watching Sara as she frantically dries and dresses. Once ready to go out, Sara, almost orders Lada to move and dress herself, Lada reluctantly obeys. Then they both hurry out of the office, Sara greets Lada with a hasty kiss on the lips, and rushes like lightning to her family. As soon as she returns home, she enters in silence because all the lights are off. She goes to the kitchen and eats something, she was fasting, and they had skipped dinner. Then she looks into Sara J's bedroom who sleeps peacefully and finally goes to her room, where she sees the silhouette of Amina under the covers sleeping on her side. Fortunately, Amina turns her back on the side of Sara's bed. She undresses in silence and slips under the covers still thinking of Lada and regretting having left her so in a hurry. Amina pretends to sleep, but a tear runs down her face. This time Sara is more and more involved in her new adventure, and for her part, Lada gives herself to Sara totally. Amina suspects something, but does not react, knows that it is impossible to straighten a crooked tree, and decides to adapt herself "to the tree". She loves Sara very much, to the point of wanting to see her always happy, even if it means being betrayed, indeed sexual betrayal has no value for a couple that is united by love. She does not realize, however, that her life begins to be increasingly mutilated of an important and fundamental part of it: Sara's attentions towards her. Amina is increasingly committed to work, extending her working hours. The owner has a soft spot for her; he welcomed her like a sister. His name is Alì, and he came to London with his parents when he was twenty years old. He soon managed to set aside money with the help of his father and took over a pub that was about to fail. Since Alì became the owner of the pub he wanted to be called John and no longer Alì, but since then, in spite of himself, his name for everyone has become Johnalì. He met a Scottish woman about ten years older than him, and married her shortly before opening the pub. Indeed, the money of his Scottish wife, Andrea, gave the final push for the pub. Their marital ménage is solid and lasting, but the wife, after the first years of marriage, has stopped seeing in her husband the ideal partner, and although she never has conflicts with him, she gradually moved away from the pub, stopping to help in the affairs of the pub. Now Amina has entered. Her docility and loyalty impressed Johnalì, who gave her more and more space in the pub. Amina, to make up unconsciously for Sara's lack of presence, begins to take an interest again in the fate of her sister Anbar. She doesn't even know if she got married, if she has problems! Then she also thinks of her family, now it's been four years since she ran away and her father and brother are always fugitives. She begins to believe that there would be nothing wrong if she calls her cousin Alif, at least he has always been her friend, and then he could give her news of the dear sister Anbar. She wants to know if Alif has suffered any consequences for her escape, if her ex-husband has remarried! Yet she gives up, she knows it would be too dangerous if they learned where she and Sara live. These intents of Amina are set aside when, unexpectedly Johnalì, the owner of the pub, decides to share with her the management of the business. He is tired, and wants to devote some time to himself, so he offers Amina half the license and therefore the management of the pub. Amina gladly accepts she considers this offer as her desired emancipation since she first came to Italy, when she was still a minor. Returning home, while she is on the subway, she cannot wait to tell Sara this wonderful news. She remembers her first landing in Italy, the first times she met Sara at the tables of the bar in Palermo. She is moved, she loves Sara very much, indeed a lot. She hopes that by becoming an entrepreneur she will be able to attract her attention again. Sara in the meantime is increasingly involved in the story with Lada, now in the office everyone knows about this relationship. It seems that Sara has lost all inhibitory brakes, but in reality, she has managed to keep her work separate from her private life. The evening when Amina runs home to give the good news to Sara it is the anniversary of the first time Sara and Lada have been together. Sara has no plans to return soon, she wants to spend a pleasant evening with Lada. As always, she comes up with an excuse, always the usual one: she had a mishap at work. When Amina returns home, she finds Sara J still with the babysitter, she grows gloomy, and the girl informs her that Mrs. Sara has phoned to beg her to stay at least until Amina returns, since she had a mishap at work. Amina is furious, "Now she doesn't even call me anymore to warn me that she remains out with her whores, we got to the point that I need to know from the babysitter". She is disappointed, nervous. She wonders what advantage she has from this new role at work if she has lost the love or perhaps the consideration of Sara! Then she calms down, prepares food for Sara J and realizes that Sara actually loves her, but she is made like that. She would like to go to bed quite late, she hopes to meet Sara on her return, but then decides not to wait, indeed better if she does not meet her, they could argue irretrievably. As always, she lies on her side, turning her back on Sara's part of the bed and waiting for her partner to return before falling asleep.

The following day, Saturday, Amina gets up early despite not having slept throughout the night. She was awake when Sara came back at 2 a.m., "How cheeky," she thinks. However, her love always prevails; she prepares the breakfast for the two Sara, wants to give the good news with a good breakfast. The little girl now is five and a half years old, wakes up early and helps her mother to prepare breakfast, perhaps slowing her down due to her childish inexperience. Finally, both of them go to the bedroom. Sara wakes up groggy, she has been late for "work", and as soon as she sees her two women with the breakfast tray well set, she marvels and a little dismayed fears that she has forgotten about some anniversary! She remains dumbfounded until Amina tells her the good news. Sara is in seventh heaven, radiant. She decides that all three, today, will go out for the whole day: carousel, lunch out, then skating rink, where Sara J other times has proved to be a good skater. Amina won't believe this: Sara has decided to dedicate a whole day to the family as she once did! The day passes just as planned, the most carefree and happy is Sara J. Amina knows well that her partner will not repeat the same day forever. Sara, throughout the day, thought a little bit about Lada too. At the end of the day, they are tired, so they buy candlelit dinner outside and consume it at home. Sara repeats that at least one day a week they will repeat a day like this. Amina is very satisfied: it seems that Sara really had fun, completely passionate with them throughout the day. Sara is very happy with how things are going in Amina's life; she always loves her very much, and actively participates in her new experience. She goes more often to the pub, now run by her wife, and intervenes more actively in the family ménage. The two women return to be more serene, at least Amina, satisfied with the greater time Sara spends with her, now she is sure that Sara no longer considers her as a boring lover, but as an energetic entrepreneur. In reality, Amina without realizing it, changes totally: she begins to assert herself more at home, while before it was usually only Sara to make every decision. They also begin to attend Johnalì and Andrea; they often exchange visits and dinners. Sara becomes familiar with Andrea; she considers her a very independent and outgoing woman. Amina hopes that Sara will not ruin everything, but this time Sara is sincerely and favorably fascinated by Andrea, without any hidden purpose. The four forge an increasingly solid friendship, dragged by the fraternal affection that Johnalì feels for Amina. Andrea and Johnalì have twins who now, at the age of twenty, have gone to enlist in the army; they have not assumed their father's role by helping him in the pub. Also, for this reason, Johnalì was looking for a helper, fortunately finding him in Amina. Later, due to the new commitments, the days that the family had promised to spend entirely away from home, will be repeated very few times. Amina changes her working hours and she doesn't have much free time anymore. Unfortunately, without noticing, they lose a habit dear to them, the one that has had a prominent place in their lives: there is no longer that little tune whistled almost every night. Amina, having changed working hours, very often returns home tired and destroyed only after 10.30. Only Sara J notices the lack of this daily ritual. An important piece of their lives was lost along with the tune whistled by Amina.

One afternoon Sara returns from work upset, she is alone at home, Sara J is at her friend's and Amina is at work. She is dismayed and upset. Lada's husband came to work, made a rebuke and shouted in front of everyone in the office his anger at having discovered his wife's secret love affair. Sara was humiliated, Lada went away with her husband avoiding all the time to meet Sara's gaze. Since that day, she has never returned to work. The husband revealed everything, offending and humiliating Sara, and not his wife, whom he considers a victim. Sara realized that Lada blamed only her. The man also claimed that Sara raped her, and by leaving, he threatened to sue her. However, Sara does not believe that it will be possible to take her to court; everyone in the office knew this relationship and this would have gone in her favor. On the other hand, inevitably this great scandal perhaps will have consequences. The next day Sara decides that she will not pretend nothing has happened at work, if she did, she would show weakness, as well as shame for her Sapphic love. She courageously gathers her colleagues and publicly apologizes to everyone for what happened. In this way, she shows great pride and dignity. She explains that she has made a mistake that she will treasure, but she adds that above all she has been wrong in the evaluation of the person. She begs her colleagues to forgive her again and to consider her as the collaborator of all time. She does not mention homosexuality, and this puts her on a higher step than the chatter and gossip that are often unleashed even with caricature and arrogant tones towards Sapphic love. Her speech, devoid of any sense of guilt but which expresses only regret for the events, causes a sensation among colleagues. Everyone is close to her and blames Lada's crazy husband. Nevertheless, if someone dares to blame Lada, Sara demonstrates her dignity even more by asking not to blame Lada, who by the way is no longer present among them. This attitude exonerates her from disciplinary measures, and everything returns as before, even better than before. Sara is now totally accepted by all her colleagues even by those who for religion, culture and other reasons considered her a deviant woman.

Meanwhile, Amina is increasingly satisfied working at the pub, she is enthusiastic, even if she is forced to spend less and less time with the two women in her family. She seems to have temporarily put aside her desire to see her family again. However, day after day, month after month, that project, relegated to a drawer, constantly returns to peep. Sara J is now six years old, the same years since they moved to London. Italian justice has not yet indicted those responsible for her kidnapping, Italian lawyers have told that unfortunately the inquisitive people are partly fugitives. Her husband is a fugitive so as not to be extradited from his country to Italy, while his brother and father have managed to avoid extradition, for the moment. Amina's thoughts go to her younger sister, Anbar, who is now supposed to be a mother. She would like to know her children, indeed, she would like Anbar to come to London, with her working position in the pub, she could easily offer her sister a chance. Sometimes she imagines that Anbar doesn't get along with her husband and consequently would have the desire to escape too! Maybe Amina just wants to fill a void in her life; Sara is unable to show that unique and exclusive affection for her wife, even though she always returns home methodically without deviating to other paths, especially after the Lada scandal. On the other hand, Amina never knew anything about the Lada scandal, but Sara has well learned the lesson, she has also fortunately avoided a lawsuit for rape that would have had serious repercussions on her family life. The ritual of the evening whistle is no longer repeated, a further indication of a loosening of their bond. Little Sara J occupies all their energy, now she goes to school: the first homework, the first classmates.

One evening, after dinner, while Sara J is in her room with a friend, Amina reveals to Sara the desire to resume contact with her mother and sister. She would like to know how things are going! Sara wince, is stunned, then warns her: "Are you crazy? Are you a moron? After all they've done to you, do you still meditate about them? After the dangers, we ran to come and save you, do you still think about that gang of criminals? I remember that you are in dispute with them". Amina is silent, she prefers not to answer, but Sara realizes that she has replied abruptly and knows that the embers under the ashes will continue to burn despite all. From that evening on, Sara keeps an eye on Amina; she would like to avoid a gesture without consent. She is convinced that Amina can stupidly call someone in her country and reveal their address; indeed, until then, for security reasons, they had totally avoided, even in the official acts of the trial, to reveal their residence. Amina seems to accept Sara's advice, works and continues her life, works and continues her marriage ménage and her responsibilities as the mother of a beautiful child. One day, being at home for a slight flu, she looks for Alif's number. "Well, she thinks, six years have passed, maybe he won't want to know about me, and indeed I betrayed him when I ran away without his knowledge". She is undecided; she has Alif's number in front of her. Finally, dial the number. The phone rings, rings but nothing, then after many more rings she hears the voice of Alif who answers in English, "What stupid I am she thinks, Alif has seen that the number comes from the United Kingdom, now it is no longer possible for me to hide our residence". She does not lose heart; first, she greets Alif, and then asks him if he can speak, if he is alone! Alif is silent, remains silent, while Amina hears as if he is opening a lock and closing a door, and then hears the noise of traffic. Alif went to the street, now he is free to speak, "Amina, is it you? How are you?", and Amina, "Well well, but how are you?", "I'm fine too", he is excited. Without wasting time, he tells her that he has recently married a good girl, who is pregnant with her first child, a boy. Amina is moved, the dear cousin still loves her, "Dear Alif,

I have always had regret for having deceived you and left you alone with my former sister-in-law, have you forgiven me?" Alif also moved, "Of course, you have no fault; I was in pain for you when they forced you to marry. However, don't worry, I'm not involved in your escape, no one knew that I unintentionally helped you, only that fool of your former sister-in-law was punished for not watching over you. Unfortunately, your family members, your father and your brothers hate you. Your husband, since you ran away, has disappeared to avoid the consequences of the international cause you have unleashed. Yet that pig deserves it. Unfortunately, you have to know that he also swore revenge". Amina is not afraid, she is sure that her ex-husband is harmless, forced to hide so as not to be arrested, "Alif I am glad that you still love me, and, believe me, I feel sorry for my family. I hurt them, but I had no other choice, that bad man of my husband deserved everything as perhaps my brother Adel also deserved it", Alif interrupts her, "To be honest, maybe only Adel didn't forgive you, but I think your father misses you. He became very old after your escape and its consequences. You must know that a terrible scandal broke out here, fortunately, Anbar had already married, otherwise she would have had no chance to do so. By the way, your ex-husband remarried, he also obtained the annulment of your marriage after filing a complaint against you for abandonment of the marital home, and then he married a fool worthy of him. However, immediately after filing his complaint against you, the Court then annuls his complaint, he was forced to hide and change his name in order not to be reached by law. I know where he lives, but I can't say it so as not to get into trouble. You have to know that that villain is still in contact with Adel and they both want to take a revenge. Your legal action against them forces them into hiding and ... and.... Adel has also changed his name, so both live under false generalities. In any case, Adel will never be able to return to Italy except as an illegal immigrant. In the event that someone will stop him, if he still tries to enter Italy, they will arrest him immediately because they have his fingerprints". Amina is satisfied with this phone call, and asks Alif if he can give Anbar's phone, she wants to talk to her too. Alif replies that he must ask because since all this trouble happened, the family of Anbar's husband no longer wants any contact with them and has forbidden his wife to have any contact. Then Amina tells Alif about the birth of Sara J, the only beautiful gift she received from that cursed one. She tells him that she loves the little girl and that she grows up very well with Sara's help. She would like to talk to him about her marriage, but perhaps Alif is not prepared for news like this, so she prefers to keep quiet. Alif is very surprised by the birth of Sara J; he had no idea that Amina was pregnant when she ran away. Indeed, the husband did not disclose this news, otherwise he would have been induced to take back the child who was about to be born; according to their custom, children should live with their father. The two say goodbye, but it is understood that Amina will call back to get her sister's number, indeed she begs Alif to prepare Anbar for this phone call so as not to surprise her. Amina prefers not to tell Sara about the phone call, she knows she would disapprove. Amina is convinced that she can reconnect at least with her mother and sister, if not with her father. Life goes on, but Sara is increasingly suspicious. Finally, after a few days Amina manages to get the phone of Anbar, which is of the mother-in-law, since Anbar, after the scandal of her sister, is not allowed to have a phone of her own. However, the mother-in-law does not know how to use it well, and then has eye problems that forcing her to wear glasses dark enough to not be able to distinguish numbers on the keyboard. One evening, the three women are on the couch watching television, Amina clearly has the thought elsewhere, Sara also pretends to follow the television programs, she also has the thought elsewhere, she thinks about some of her new achievements. Amina takes courage, "Sara?" and looks at her with doe eyes, and Sara: "What? Your eyes announce something bad to me", Amina, "I just want to tell that I managed to get my sister's phone". Sara snaps sitting on the couch, "How the hell did you manage to get it? Stupid, now they know where we are, where we live and everything else...". Amina, taking her by the hand and walking away to leave Sara J alone, leads her to the kitchen and explains in a low voice that she was not a fool, and that she spoke to Alif in secret. Sara does not want to hear excuses; she keeps repeating that she is a jerk and a reckless. Amina gets angry and locks herself in their bedroom, slamming the door behind her. Sara is furious, she sees Sara J looking into the kitchen, with a fearful look. Sara hugs her, she would like to tell her that she has a stupid mother, but simply explains that her mother is a little tired and that everything is fine. When Sara and Amina argue with each other, they do it in Italian, so Sara J doesn't understand what they say. Sara J was born and lived in London and speaks English and Amina's mother tongue quite well. The two mothers do not realize that Sara J unknowingly, little by little, listening to their private conversations, begins to understand even a little Italian. At night Sara sleeps on the sofa in the living room, indeed, she does not sleep, she has nightmares in which she sees that faceless people come to kidnap Amina and kill her. In the morning she wakes up nervous and shaken, she has breakfast ignoring Amina, and goes out quickly to work. She does nothing but think about the imprudence of Amina's behavior. She wants to do everything possible to distract her and find out what news she has revealed to Alif about their lives. Finally, she decides that if that stupid Amina wants to meet any of her family members, she will do it without Sara J, their daughter will never move away from Sara. In this Cold War, at least a couple of weeks pass during which the two women do not return to a domestic serenity. Sara always sleeps on the sofa, a choice that hurts Amina a lot, who, instead, wants to reconcile with Sara. Amina is aware that Sara has always been hard on her, and this attitude pushes her to find more and more comfort in Alif. During following conversations with Alif, Amina discovers that

Anbar is dissatisfied with her husband, and as that chatterbox Alif makes clear, Anbar is saddened by the turn her married life has taken. She too was imprisoned in the house for the first years of the marriage, due to the scandal of her family and is practically submissive to her husband's family. She had two children, and her husband intends to have a third. Amina is very sorry for her sister's difficulties, especially since they are caused by her rebellion and escape. She remembers when the two sisters confided in each other their desires for the future; Anbar always confirmed that she wanted to study and become a doctor, and that she would not want to have children. These memories afflict Amina, and the desire to help her sister is increasingly manifested in her. From her point of view, it would be relatively simple: it would be enough to organize a kidnapping as already done with her, but the children! The two sons will not follow their mother if they are fond of their father, as Alif mentioned! Amina realizes that she is fantasizing but wants to contact her sister. The propitious moment comes when Anbar has communicated to Alif the precise day when she is alone at home with her mother-in-law, the time when her mother-in-law goes for an afternoon nap, leaving her cell phone unattended. While waiting for her sister's call, Anbar turns down the cell phone ringer completely, feverishly awaiting the call. Amina also organizes herself, trying to be alone, not in the presence of Sara, nor of Sara J. Everything seems organized, Amina is at work, so she goes out on the street and dials the number. It rings, almost immediately replies the sister who is evidently in fervent expectation. They don't greet each other; they barely call each other by name to make sure they're right on the phone. They both cry for emotion after so many years. Amina asks how she is, if she likes her life, Anbar does not answer questions, but in turn asks Amina how she is. As long as the emotion gives them respite, then the two sisters tell all the latest events of their lives, always in a low voice, the mother-in-law could wake up. Anbar reassures her sister that she is well and satisfied with her life, but Amina knows she is telling a lie. She asks if they can meet somewhere, but it seems impossible. Amina cannot return to her country, and how can Anbar ever reach Italy or the United Kingdom? Amina tells about Sara J and her love for the little girl. But in her conversation, she neglects to mention her marriage to Sara, she thinks it's best not to reveal it for the moment, maybe one day, maybe. She fears losing her sister's esteem. Their conversation must be interrupted suddenly, Anbar hears her mother-in-law coughing. Before closing the communication, both promises to organize a plan to be able to meet. Anbar deletes the phone call from the memory of the cell phone and turning up the volume, immediately puts it next to the mother-in-law, who, in the meantime, has taken a nap after coughing. Amina, on the other hand, is desolate. She misses her sister so much; she wants to give her the chance to go and live with her in London.

The meeting.

The phone calls with her sister relieve Amina so much that she makes peace with Sara. For her part, Sara would like to be sure that Amina no longer intends to meet her family. However, she remains vigilant about Amina's movements as much as she can, especially among her amorous conquests. The phone calls with her sister have also pushed Amina to confide more than usual with Johnalì, taking advantage of their long days at work, and, day after day, manages to convince Johnalì to help her. Johnalì is more cautious, and first he wants to talk to Alif, he wants to make sure that he is not deceiving Amina. Johnalì has always been protective of Amina, and now this project of his friend and colleague scares him no less than it can scare Sara. Cristian and Cris are also informed of her desire to meet Anbar, she hopes for help from them too. However, the two boys do not respond favorably, first they do not want to lie to Sara by hiding their help for this very risky plan, and at the same time, they try to dissuade her. The phone calls between Amina and Anbar go on incessantly. By now, they have figured out how to get organized: Anbar first rings her sister as soon as she finds the right moment, a single ring so as not to start the phone calls from her mother-in-law's phone, and then Amina calls her back immediately. Anbar confesses to her sister that she couldn't resist, that she revealed to her mother, Raissa, the birth of Sara J, and Raissa was moved. Perhaps Anbar should not have reported this news to her mother, Amina meditates, and it is a risk to let her know that she also has a daughter from her ex-husband. She asks her sister what her mother's reaction was! Unfortunately, Anbar does not want to answer, then gives up and confesses her regret, her mother was moved at first, but she then added that it would be right if the child grew up with her father. Amina is irritated by her mother's response; she has the confirmation that maternal love cannot overcome certain traditions. However, after about a month, Anbar tells her that she visited her parents accompanied by her husband, two children, father-in-law and mother-in-law. An unscheduled visit, even if the two families have recently begun to meet at least on national and religious holidays. During the family reunion, males preferred to get together alone to talk to each other about business and money matters, at least as they said. They stayed with her parents for a long time, more than usual. Upon return, her husband was taciturn, then, once they got home, he finally revealed to her that Anbar's father asked him to go and visit his son who lives in France. He would like Anbar's husband and his son who immigrated to France to start a trade together, one not well defined. Finally, the two sisters understand that this is a good opportunity to meet. Amina passionately resumes devising a plan; if her sister really comes to France, she does not intend to miss this opportunity. In subsequent telephone calls, Anima communicates to her sister the decision to join her in France, in the province of Marseille, where their brother lives. Amina and Anbar are sure that somehow, they will be able to meet; they just have to define the details. They will both be geographically very close in the European Union, so why not take advantage! Anbar should walk away alone, without even the children, and secretly meet Amina. "It's impossible, Anbar replies, someone will have to accompany me wherever I want to go, my husband would never let me out alone". Amina suggests that she run away with her children and take refuge with her. Anbar explains to her that the two children are very close to their father, and that she loves them so much that she never leaves them, just as the two children would never leave their father. Waiting for this trip, the two sisters continue to call each other almost regularly when the old woman takes her afternoon nap. Amina confides only in Johnalì, who for his part follows her systematically. The events accelerate, Anbar finally communicates to her sister the day set for the trip, and it is next month, which is April, on 20th. Even her husband is proceeding with visas and plane tickets. The decisions to take become much more feverish and the two sisters must organize themselves quickly. Eventually they decide that Anbar will pretend to want to meet a friend of hers, Marianna, Carlo's wife, who met her just when Amina visited their home. Anbar knows that she will have to go out at least with her children, never alone. This is a decisive first step for their meeting. Therefore, Marianna's presence is necessary and Amina will do everything possible to convince her. So, Amina will come to the meeting in the company of Marianna, but she will be disguised. Anbar's children do not know their aunt, and therefore Amina can introduce herself together with Marianna but as the wife of ... but of whom...? Then it comes to her mind, but yes, of Johnalì. He will also come to this meeting so he can pretend to be her husband. With this plan, she will not even have to disturb the two Cristian. Well, everything seems organized, although not for the best. Only now, once Anbar's journey has been established, Amina takes courage and reveals to Sara all the last phone calls with her sister. As expected, Sara gets angry and screams like never before, but she also realizes that his partner is determined and doesn't want to reconsider. She insults Amina and reiterates that she does not want to enter into this affair, that now Amina has to face it alone, and that this time she will not come to save her. Amina tries to calm her down, explains that she will not be alone, but that there will be Johnalì, and Carlo and Marianna will also come, so she will go without any fear to the appointment. Finally, she reveals that they will meet near Marseilles, France. Sara does not want to hear excuses, not so much for the danger of this meeting, she trusts Johnalì and then objectively they will meet in French territory, but she is angry because for the first time Amina excluded her without telling her anything. For the first time she did her thing without giving weight to Sara advice. Sara is very self-centered, and to have been sidelined is the worst thing Amina could have done. Sara forgets that Amina has never objectively angered her in the twelve years they live together. Amina, however, took a weight off her shoulders, now that she has revealed everything to Sara, she feels free to go on as organized with her sister. Shortly before the eve of the trip, Anbar writes a message on Amina cell phone, tells her that they can no longer call each other because her mother-in-law always has her mobile phone in her pocket, perhaps she has noticed something. Now the way of communicating changes, it will only be Anbar to send messages with her mother-in-law's mobile phone, as soon as she manages to take it for a few seconds, but Amina must never write on her own initiative, nor can she respond to Anbar's messages. The day of departure of Anbar and family to Marseille is approaching. Amina asks Carlo and Marianna to accompany her, but unfortunately, they cannot, Marianna is pregnant again, but this time she has a pregnancy at risk, so for the first four months she must usually remain lying down without making efforts. The two Cristian, change their mind and do not want to leave their friend in trouble, so they are happy to help Amina, but the problem is that they need a female presence to replace Marianna. Fortunately, Johnalì intervenes, offering to come with his wife Andrea. Amina accepts the offer of her friend and partner, she thanks the two Cristian explaining that it will be better if they go in a few to the fateful meeting, and reassures them, "We are in French territory, in Marseille; what will happen to me!" They are already; Sara is

156

informed of everything even if she pretends not to care. Finally, on April 19, Anbar writes the last message to her sister before departure, specifying that tomorrow they will be in Marseille. She asks Amina to leave immediately for Marseille with Sara J, and be ready for the meeting, the next day, even with a minimum notice of half an hour. Anbar explains that she sensed that she could make a little escape and be able to go out alone, or with her children, at least for an hour, just to meet her and her niece Sara J. She concludes by writing that she has a great desire to know the little one and that she has a gift for her. If they are lucky, later they can meet "officially" with the cover of Anima's friends, but for this first meeting Anbar is quite optimistic to be able to see Amina alone even if only for half an hour. The last sentence she writes is, "It will be our half hour alone with Sara J, and we will remember it forever. Amina is very happy, she instructs Sara J to answer, in case she will meet her cousins, that Johnalì is her father and that her mother's name is not Amina, but Andrea, will use the name of Johnalì's wife. Therefore, Amina will introduce herself with Johnalì as her husband, she will be called Andrea, and Johnalì's real wife, Andrea, will be called Marianna, like Anbar's old friend. Everything seems organized, everyone agrees and everyone is about to leave for Marseille, to be ready for the big meeting. When Amina leaves the London apartment, at the time of leaving, only Sara J hugs Sara strongly, Amina instead, addressing her in a superficial way, "Hi Sara, we will see on our return", and Sara, with the same stunted coldness, "OK, see you soon, bye". A hesitant Amina takes Sara J, opens the door, goes out and then closes it. Sara remains alone in her pain for so much indifference created by both, she is about to despair, when she hears coming from outside, "e - C - - A A g - C - - ", She gets up happy and runs towards the front door, when she opens it the two women embrace each other tightly, moving. They do not notice to be almost in the street, in front of all the passers-by. They kiss, and Sara J is happy watching the two mothers reconciled. She also suffered from the frost that had fallen in the house. Sara stands leaning against the doorjamb as she sees Amina and Sara J get into the taxi. One last farewell and then off to the airport. Sara enters the house more relieved and happier.

The next day, April 20, everyone is waiting anxiously; also, Sara from London is waiting for news. The group that went to Marseille still does not receive any messages from Anbar; they guess that perhaps the mother-in-law did not go with them, so Anbar does not have her cell phone available. It is evening and Amina decides to go to all the hotels in Marseille to find her sister, but realizes that it would be an impossible task, and Anbar will almost certainly stay with her brother in the province of Marseille. Amina regrets that she never asked for her brother's address. Johnalì and Andrea can hardly calm her down and convince her to wait at least the next day before making any further decision. On the 21st morning, at six in the morning, a message arrives on Amina's cell phone, an unknown number, "Dear

Amina, I am Anbar, I am using this mobile because my mother-in-law's is not available. Let's see you in half an hour. I will come with my nephew and my two children; I will leave them for a moment sitting at the ice cream kiosk and I will be absent for a few minutes. Better if you come only with Sara J, so as not to attract the attention of the boys. Then she writes the directions: Parc Valmer, towards Anse de la Fausse. Describe a local bus stop. Please, she adds, only you and the child come for the moment, then we will organize ourselves better for the official meeting, the one with the consent of my husband and with the presence of Marianna and her husband. Amina quickly prepares Sara J and as she is about to leave her hotel room, Johnalì notices it and stops her, he wants to come too, better not trust Anbar. Amina is reluctant, bur then she agrees; another person is not a problem. However, it occurs to her that her sister may be angry because she has clearly specified that she will come with her two children and nephew, if the boys find out anything, could skip it all. Amina insists on Johnalì to go alone, and Johnalì pretends to consent, in reality he intends to follow his friend secretly. Amina goes out, takes a taxi. Johnalì tries to take one immediately after her, but does not have time, he lost Amina's, but he remembers the address and looks for another taxi hoping to reach her. Johnalì arrives at the agreed point late, gets out of the taxi quickly, and pays without even waiting for the rest. He looks around and catches a glimpse from a distance of Amina running at a brisk pace with the little girl close to her, while running she turns back in fear. Johnalì realizes that she is followed, indeed chased by four people. He also runs towards Amina, and while he runs, he sees Amina who, frightened, runs and turns back to check if her pursuers are reaching her. When she finally realizes that she has almost been reached, she inveighs against four men who follow her. Johnalì has a shudder of fear and while running, he decides to scream to get someone's attention, but the area is still deserted. Amina tries to hurry up by dragging the little girl closer and closer to her. The four men reach her, and exasperated by the woman's escape and screams, decide to end it. They pull out knives, grab the woman, and yank her, while one of them tries to separate the girl from her. The scuffle is violent, Johnalì observes everything while running out of breath, falls to the ground, recovers and limping tries to reach them. Three men hold the woman steady and the fourth snatches the girl from her arms. As he drags the little girl away towards a van, the other three stab Amina who emits shrill screams of terror. Finally, she falls to the ground in a pool of blood. The three killers pick her up and drag her to the van. Meanwhile, the fourth man lets the child escape from his hand and, to stop her, he throws the knife at her, hitting her in the back. The little girl also falls to the ground wounded. The man reaches her, takes her in his arms and runs away. Johnalì, is now near the aggression, he did just in time to meet the gaze of the little girl who with her hand stretched out to him, terrified, asks him for help, just before being stabbed. All the attackers manage to get into the van, which leaves before even being able to close the van's tailgate. Johnalì can only follow with his gaze which direction the van takes, while he watches horrified the pool of blood on the ground and the trail of blood up to where the van was parked. He immediately calls the police before notifying everyone else. Then he calls his wife; Andrea screams in despair, and then she rushes to the place. Johnalì is still terribly alone while waiting for the arrival of rescue, he tries to run in the direction of the van to follow its path, but loses it, he has his ankle that hurts and prevents him from running. The police record the testimony of Johnalì, delimit the area for the surveys. Meanwhile, curious people begin to rush, few, indeed, that area just before was deserted. The scene that the investigators find is terrible: a woman with her daughter were stabbed and kidnapped. The police order the search for the van and immediately issue an order for various checkpoints. They ask Johnalì and his wife, who in the meantime has joined them, to go to the police station and get in touch with the victim's family. Johnalì does not want to leave the place of the assassination, he wants to follow the developments in person, and he is convinced that they will find the van shortly thereafter; it is certainly still nearby. He insists on the cops and does not move from there. After an hour, some officers warn them that the van was found not far away, but empty. Everyone rushes to the site of the discovery and finds the van dirty with blood and empty. The police track down the owner, who had not yet noticed the theft. The owner is an elderly person who rarely uses that van. Even the phone used to confirm the appointment appears to have been stolen that same morning, always from an elderly person, who had not yet been able to report the theft. In short, the murderers, or kidnappers, were very cunning; they acted quickly and professionally. The police reveal that the mode of the crime is typical of the local mafia. They are looking for the four criminals and the bodies of the two women, although they hope they are not dead. Johnalì and his wife also participate in the search; both do not want to go to the police station. An ambulance also arrives to make sure they are well, but both refuse any treatment and they search near the van to look for traces of the two women. Finally, after about two hours, they decide that it is more useful to go to the police station and leave a more complete deposition, telling all the stories of Amina, and therefore why they had come to Marseille. The police decide to track down Amina's brother who works and lives in the province of Marseille. The police commissioner of Marseille also receives information from the Italian judge, that is, the holder of Amina's case against her brother Adel and her former husband. When they manage to track down her brother who lives near Marseilles, they immediately summon him to the police station. Meanwhile, it is evening, Sara has already phoned many times, and now Johnalì must call her to give her the bad news. Finally, he decides, he calls her. Sara hearing Johnalì's voice broken by emotion, does not wait to hear anything else, screams and falls to the ground desperately with the phone in her hand. Johnalì is silent, suffering. Then Sara asks, "Is she dead? And Sara J is dead?", and Johnalì: "They were kidnapped, they are looking for them, but there is blood in the van used for the kidnapping", does not reveal that he witnessed the scene and the stabbing of both. Sara tells him that she will reach Marseille immediately. In the evening the police receive a phone call from a passer-by who reports that he found a body floating at the base of the cliff along the bend de la Fausse. After recovering the body, the police summon Johnalì for the recognition of the body. Johnalì recognizes Amina. There are traces of blood on the cliff, evidently, the killers threw her from the road along the cliff during the escape, and probably the child suffered the same fate! Meanwhile, a massive manhunt has begun throughout the area with checkpoints. Nothing emerges from the interrogation of Amina's brother. The man swears he knows nothing about his sister Anbar's visit from their country with her husband and in-laws. He adds that he has no contact with his brother-in-law and that there was no plan to conclude a deal together, there was no reason to meet in Marseille. His alibi is perfect; he was at work very early in the morning in the machine shop where he works. The brother is cleared, but they fear that he will not tell the truth. Is he an accomplice of the gang? Did he act as a sort of mastermind? In the meantime, they ask him not to leave the city. Investigators think that one of the members of the gang could have been Amina's brother, Adel, as well as they suspect that her ex-husband was also part of the four murderers. They send a request for investigation to their colleagues in Amina's home Country, but receive negative responses, as both have been fugitives for years. The police confirm that they have changed their name and address to escape the ongoing lawsuit for the kidnapping of Amina dating back to a few years earlier. They can't even contact Anbar and her husband. They only get to contact Anbar's mother-in-law, who frightened, reports that the son with his whole family are visiting his brother in a remote area of the country. The commissioner begins to believe that they have set up a trap without the knowledge of her brother resident in Marseille and without the knowledge of her sister Anbar. The police on the other side of the Mediterranean go to the home of Amina's parents and at the same time try to reach the inaccessible area where the Anbar family is supposed to be. Police officers in Amina's Country tell their colleagues in Marseille that Amina's parents are devastated by the news of their daughter's death. They took them to the police station for questioning and, despite their age, the local police decide not to leave them until they manage to extort further information. The night is spent waiting for further developments and in the constant search for the child's body, when, the next morning, Sara arrives. She goes directly to the police station, without first meeting Johnali, she wants to see Amina's body. The police take her to the morgue. As soon as Sara finds herself in front of Amina's body, battered, stained with blood and with her face swollen from falling on the rocks, she gently touches the face of Amina, with a delicate and desperate gesture; then she faints. They take her to the hospital, where Johnalì joins her; he stays at her bedside until she wakes up. As soon as she comes to herself, they embrace, but Sara no longer has contact with reality, she looks to be narcotized, her gaze is lost in the void. She answers questions late, so much so that Johnalì asks if she has been narcotized! Doctor answer that they only injected her with a drip to hydrate her; they had noticed that she had not drunk and had been eating for more than twenty hours. Sara has entered a world separate from everyone else's, only comes back to herself when she asks about Sara J. The investigation continues. From the police station on the other side of the Mediterranean comes further news: Anbar was joined by the local police and was heard with her husband. They report that Anbar was desperate at the news of her sister's death and that she lashed out at her husband accusing him of deceiving her and killing her sister. The woman, as she put on record, reported that her husband had noticed the phone calls between her and Amina, and had evidently reported everything to Adel. Then Anbar speculated that her husband and brother Adel arranged to set a trap for Amina. Anbar also explained to the police that she and her sister regularly spoke over the phone, but secretly via her mother-in-law's cell phone. Then her husband made her believe she was going to Marseille. The departure had been set for April 20, but the day before, on April 19, the husband put all of them in the car to go to his brother's house, in a remote place in the desert. Anbar believed in a sudden change of program, and was not alarmed, but she could no longer contact her sister, no longer having a mobile phone available. Moreover, when she asked her husband about the trip, he reassured her by answering that everything had been postponed. Unfortunately, she could not notify her sister of the change of program because she had no possibility to call and had no internet connection available in that remote place where her husband had led them. Everything seems terribly outlined: Anbar's husband has a sure alibi, having gone with his family to his brother's house in that remote area of the country. The investigators are sure that he is one of the accomplices who organized the fake trip to trap Amina, through her sister Anbar who was unaware of everything. From France they ask their overseas colleagues to stop the man for further investigation. Then the man is detained on charges of complicity and interrogate him to extort the names of the four murderers who came to Marseille; who is the principal and organizer of the whole operation. Meanwhile, Sara does not participate in the investigation; she simply answers the commissioner's questions. She became like a survivor of a storm that sank her ship with all her memories and affections. Her friends realize that Sara has unconsciously detached herself from them, as if she no longer feels any feeling of friendship for anyone. They understand that she is traumatized and suggest that she return to London with Andrea. Johnalì wants to test on the spot to follow the developments and above all, he too is engaged in the feverish search for the child. The police begin to be hesitant, if the child is not dead, surely, she will have been kidnapped, but for what purpose? They speculate that it was revenge on Amina's ex-husband for leaving him and suing him. Investigators confirm that there is very little hope of finding the child alive. According to Johnalì's testimony, the child had wriggled out and, while escaping, was stopped by the knife thrown by one of the killers, who hit her in the back. Sara does not know these details; they thought it was better not to tell her anything about the child. Even after the investigation is over, Sara will not learn of the brutal throwing of the knife behind the child; they decide it's too cruel scene. The following day the two Cristian also arrive, they are destroyed by pain; Sara J is their daughter. A few more days pass, and on the other side of the Mediterranean no further news is received. Anbar's husband continues to deny any involvement, so does her brother who emigrated to Marseille. However, while there are serious suspicions about Anbar's husband for complicity, so they continue to hold him back, as for the brother of Marseilles there is no evidence or any element about him for his involvement in these two murders. Now there is clear talk of two murders. Amina's brother Adel and her ex-husband are always on the run, though investigators hope Amina's parents can reveal their new identity and residence. Johnalì decides never to tell Sara that he also saw the child attacked, he does not want her to know the brutal way in which the murder took place.

Everyone tries to convince Sara to return to London and follow the investigation from there. Sara does not react; the Sara of a few days before had died together with her partner and daughter. Her mind cannot decipher and integrate the present, she deludes herself that she still lives in the recent past, and her attitude is similar to a narcotized person. When they can finally take Amina's body, they decide to cremate it in Marseille. However, they have to wait two days for their turn. In those two days, Sara is the center of everyone's attention: all of them are heartbroken and disoriented. They can't believe that such a tragedy has happened; only a few days before they were all calm and happy and then, suddenly their world collapsed. Life has changed for all of them; from that moment on it will never be the same. On the day of cremation, no one can hold back the tears of despair. The ceremony takes place quickly, and at the time of putting the ashes in the small urn, Sara decides to buy another, engraved with the name of Sara J, and bring them both with her: one full and the other empty. In conclusion, everyone leaves Marseille, to go directly to Florence. The burial ceremony of the two urns in Sara's family tomb, where her parents are located, is even more heartbreaking than the cremation. Sara decided to leave her young family in the monumental cemetery of Florence; at least there are her roots. Marianna is also present at the burial, but she resists little, she faints almost immediately from pain, Amina was her dearest friend. Everyone fears for her; indeed, it was a mistake to come in her condition, she should have a caesarean section shortly after some months. That night Sara stays at the home of the two Cristian, and the next day she leaves in silence. She is not alone; Johnalì and Andrea are with her. Johnalì does not forgive himself for leaving Amina at the appointment alone, even though he had decided to follow her closely. Sara explained to him that it was not his fault, she knows that the only culprit is herself: she should never have let Amina go alone.

Once in London, they decide that Sara will go to live in her house, among her things, but Andrea will move in as long as necessary. Cris also manages to free himself from work for a couple of weeks and he also goes to Sara's house. However, life has changed for everyone, even the customers of the pub are shaken: they wish Amina was still there with them. After two weeks, Cris must return to Florence, he asks Sara if she wants to go with him, but Sara is obsessed with Amina's memories in Florence. In this city they spent perhaps the most carefree period of their lives. Sara worries everyone, she obsessively repeats all the words she didn't say to Amina, all the caresses she didn't do, and all she could have done to be closer to her now dead partner. She wonders if she had never gone to that bar in Palermo twelve years before! If she had never met her, Amina would now be alive. Sara blames herself for dragging Amina into a life far from her family, from her people, "Maybe it would have been better for her never to have met me", she repeats repeatedly.

The days pass, and unfortunately no news from

the investigations; it seems that everything ended in nothingness. No new revelation from Amina's family, indeed, the sister seems to have retracted everything. Probably Anbar was forced to retract so as not to be repudiated and remain alone in the street also expelled from her parents' house. All this increases Sara's anger; she remembers when she went to take back her woman. She would like to return to Amina's Country and carry out a massacre, then free Anbar, and take her to London to her home. Then she realizes that she has already destroyed the life of a girl, she does not want to destroy another, assuming that Anbar wants to follow her. On the other hand, Anbar knows nothing about Sara and Amina's relationship; perhaps, if she did, she might even hate both her sister and Sara. One evening, Andrea, still a guest with Sara, while arranging the blankets, accidentally finds a forgotten box in a corner of the wardrobe. She opens it and finds a series of folding knives of all sizes. She asks Sarah what they were! The woman confesses that she had bought them to take them to Amina's Country and kill Adel and Amina's ex-husband. Andrea seizes the box and tries to convince her of the uselessness of revenge, and clearly reiterates that now Amina and Sara J will never return. Sara remains paralyzed all night until the next morning. Andrea calls Johnalì, who advises against calling a doctor. The next morning, Sara feels different, as if she were a new person; the Sara of the days just passed seems to have vanished. All she has left is a veil of fog that can be glimpsed in her eyes. She is willing to resume her life, a life she believed lost forever. Andrea decides to stay for another month to keep her friend company. Sara, although she has sufficiently recovered, still lives like in a dark well, with little confidence for the future. She hates herself for how she treated Amina in the last period, before her departure for Marseille. Eventually her friends' efforts finally convince her to go to a psychologist for therapy. Little by little, Andrea returns to her house, and the two Cristian come when they can to visit her. Carlo also comes to visit her in London, Marianna has recently given birth, and she has shortly moved to her mother's house with her first child and the new baby.

That terrible summer of 2018 finally goes away, and autumn comes. Sara begins to spend more and more time in the pub where Amina worked, indeed, she has inherited half pub license, and for both entertainment and company, she starts spending all her free time working in the pub. She tries to be constantly busy; when she is free from her work, she rushes into the pub. Andrea and Johnalì are happy because they realize that Sara begins to react. Indeed, Sara returns to her normality, even if no one identifies in her a genuine happiness. When she jokes and shows that she is happy, she only does it to please others. With the arrival of the new year, Sara decides to go to Florence alone. She needs to return for a few days to the city that witnessed her love for Amina, their first home. She especially wants to go to the family grave; she realizes that has made a mistake in leaving Amina's ashes so far from her. During the trip, she will decide whether to take them to London. Often, when she is alone at home, she talks with Amina and with little Sara J, but she does so by turning her eyes towards nowhere. On the other hand, having the ashes, she could caress them and talk to them. Her greatest pain is the lack of Sara J's body. It would certainly be more encouraging for her to have at least the comfort of having her ashes. Sara J's total absence exacerbates her pain.

During the first days of her stay in Florence, she decided to be alone, later she will meet friends. However, seeing them again without Amina has a bitter taste. Now the New Year has entered a month ago, and Sara has already communicated her intention to go to Florence to Johnalì and Andrea. The couple are worried above all about her decision to be alone at least for the first few days, so they decide to warn both Cristian, Carlo and Marianna, of Sara's arrival, just to keep them alert if something should happen. Nevertheless, Sara herself decides to notify her friends of her arrival in Florence, communicating that she will get in touch with them after a few days. She claims to want to relax and see Florence again as a tourist, pretending to be a tourist. On the day of departure, the air is particularly cold in London; Sara greets and embraces Johnalì and Andrea on the platform between the tracks. She decided to go by train because she prefers to be among the people, not alone locked in the car. She doesn't even want to take a short trip by taking a plane.

The return.

I'm going home, my old happy years home. I hope that the train collects an impossible delay, so much so that it prevents me from arriving at my destination. I go back to where the memories await me greedily; lost in the alleys, forever hidden in the bowels. They are my only relatives, the only ones with which I would like to be in company".

Thus begins the first page of this story.

Sara is in Florence, upset for witnessing the woman's assault with the child in the church of Saint Lorenzo. Frustrated by the attitude of the police who believe her to be crazy or suffering from Stendhal syndrome. Then, that strange man who seems to follow her, and whom she met again, the night before, in the restaurant just in front of her hotel...

This morning she got up late. She is still upset about meeting that strange man at the restaurant the night before. Like a fearful fool, instead of facing him, she chose to run away. It is not in her nature to run away, but she feels lonely, not understood and not even protected by the police. No trace or evidence of the assault she witnessed was found.

By now, it is late in the morning, and to relax she wants to soak in the bathtub. She stays in the tub

173

until lunchtime, and then decides to return to the restaurant from which she had left in a hurry the night before. She first wants to apologize for leaving fleeing, then she wants to have lunch, and above all, she hopes to meet that strange man again. If it is true that he is following her, she will meet him again; the night brought her courage, now she is ready to fight. As soon as she enters the restaurant, she heads directly to the cash desk to apologize. The waiter of the night before is not there, it is not his shift, but the owners recognize her and reassure her that nothing happened to them. Sara sits at a table near the entrance, calmly orders her lunch, and eats slowly to pass the time. About an hour has now passed and not even the shadow of that man has appeared. After lunch, she lingers to drink coffee and browse the internet from her mobile phone. She gets bored; it occurs to her that it would be time to call the two Cristian! However, thinking about it better, she decides to postpone, she does not want to involve them in this strange new story, at least until she has come to terms with it herself. After all that has happened, she doesn't always want to be the one who creates problems and dangerous situations. While she is undecided about what to do, whether to wait any longer or leave, the man finally enters. This time Sara looks at him defiantly. She is about to get up and go directly to him to put an end to her fear, but the man precedes her. As soon as he enters the restaurant, he immediately notices Sara sitting near the entrance, and decides to go directly to her. Sara falls into terror again; she did not expect him to go to meet her, and who knows with which intentions! He might even stab her! Perhaps he himself killed the unfortunate woman with the baby. She wants to scream, takes a last deep breath and then grabs the bag to defend herself from a possible stab. Her fear lasts a few seconds, the man unexpectedly shows great kindness and courtesy, "Madam, excuse me, I think you noticed that yesterday I was also near your hotel?" Sara interrupts him angrily, "You came to my hotel to ask about me and you didn't even say who you are. How dare you, who are you! What do you want? you have tired me". As she speaks, her legs are still shaking. "Madam, calm down, I'm here to help you, I'm a police collaborator". Sara does not believe it, she fears he is a hitman, she looks at him with skepticism and holds her handbag tightly on her chest, stiffened, expecting a stab wound. The man continues, "From time to time, I am called to the service of ..." Then he suddenly keeps silent, as if he were about to reveal something strange or at least something that he knows that the interlocutor would not have accepted easily; then continues, "I'm a medium, don't worry I'm not telling you a lie. I know that for many people fortunetellers, seers, mediums are indiscriminately scammers, and I must say that sometimes it is true. However, it is also true that the police, when they no longer have the means or the hopes to solve a case, I mean a striking case; they consult us specialists in the astrological arts. We actually perceive, we sense a vision, and then we report it to the police.

Believe me, please, I have no intention of taking advantage of you or harming you". He doesn't stop talking that he hands Sara his business card and shows her also his documents. Sara, who until then was still holding her breath and clutching her handbag to her chest, now exhales the breath, deflating. She carefully reads the business card and documents and ultimately, she calms down completely. Now she is skeptical and does not give much credit and importance to her interlocutor. She actually despises him for causing her so much fear, but she remains silent. The man asks her if he can sit down for a moment to explain himself better. Now Sara knows the man's identity, so she has no longer any interest in him. She doesn't want to waste time listening to him; from fear of him she has moved on to suspicion that he wants to rob her or take advantage of her. She has never believed in magic, ghosts, witchcraft and things like that, so this person has no value in her eyes. She does not protest when the man sits down without first waiting for her consent. She remains silent; she doesn't know what to say. Then the man begins to explain, "I was at the police station when I heard about your case. Believe me; I immediately had a feeling, yes, a kind of vision". Sara still has little interest in him, and does not encourage him to move forward, nevertheless the man continues, "I got the exact feeling that what you saw actually happened ...", Sara interrupts him, "That's enough, what do you want from me? Why are you bothering me? If you got this feeling, as you say, why didn't you report it to the police immediately?

176

Why have you been silent? Now why you come here, for what reason? What do you want?" The man doesn't get angry, but he gets a little irritated, "Madam, I don't want anything from you, I tried to report my feeling to the police, but the police didn't listen to me. They hardly and rarely listen to us, as I told you. They do it only for rare and important cases". Then rising to leave, he turns to Sara one last time, "Madam; I confirm that the feeling I had is that of a fact that really happened, and I am referring to the attack you witnessed. The police are convinced that you had Stendhal's syndrome, but I don't understand these things. How I reported it to the police, and how I repeat it to you now". Sara, "How! Why if the police didn't believe you, why should I believe you? There is no trace of blood, there are no witnesses, the hit to the head they told me I took it falling to the ground unconscious, there is no evidence, damn, and how you can be sure?". The man decides to leave, but first ads, "You know that the attack was real, that it really happened. I can't even explain it to myself because there is no trace, but you know that the attack really happened". Therefore, he turns around and goes away showing that he no longer wants to talk to Sara, perhaps believing that he has been too insulted by the woman. Sara remains alone, looking into nothingness, absorbed in the memory of that horrendous aggression. All this makes no sense, there is no evidence of any kind ... Nothing at all ... She returns shaken to the hotel, and lies on the bed, she would like to take a decision, but she does not know whether to contact again that specialist in "astrological arts", as he called himself! She has his business card. Sara continues to be convinced that she really witnessed that aggression in carnival dress, and until now, only that man has confirmed to her, even if in a strange way, that that aggression has really happened for him too. She has decided, she wants to meet him, but she is afraid that it is just a trick to ask her for money. Thus, she considers going first to the police to ask about this astrologer, and then contacting him, but only after getting reassurances from the police. She leaves quickly, it's almost time for the offices to close, she hopes to arrive before the police commissioner leaves. She arrives frantically, asking about the police commissioner who had followed her case. Luckily, he's in the office. The Commissioner is amazed to see her again and hopes that it is not yet for her visions. Sara tells him about the meeting with the astrologer, but listening to his story, the commissioner is furious. He explains that these people are not allowed to talk to those involved in a court case. Now he will call him and give him a bad time. However, Sara calms him down and manages to make him desist from his intent. She explains to him that this astrologer has only confirmed what she was already sure of, and that she wishes to meet him again. She begs the commissioner to do nothing, but to give her this opportunity to talk to that man. The commissioner calms down; in the end, he can do very little. Before leaving, he advises Sara to call if this man asks for money. Sara thanks him; this unexpected help comforts her. As soon as she goes out, wasting no time, she immediately calls Ivan, this is the name written on his business card. Ivan replies that he is busy now, and he can meet her after dinner, not in Sara's hotel, but in a club, even a bar. They confirm the appointment for 8.00 p.m. that same day, so Sara goes to have dinner directly in the restaurant of the appointment. She orders a frugal dinner and then waits sitting at the table, deceiving time by answering some emails on her mobile phone. Finally, Ivan arrives. The man approaches with a little fear, but happy to finally be believed. Sara makes him sit down and they order something for both of them, only to keep occupying the table. She begins to speak, "I hope you have guessed the reason for my phone call! I say that I don't believe what you told me the first time, I don't believe in astrologers, in magic and all this stuff. Indeed, ... Indeed ... I am increasingly convinced that the attack really took place. Nobody takes this certainty out of my head. Otherwise, it would mean that I'm going crazy". After a short break during which Ivan remains silent, she continues, "I lived those terrible moments, although it is true that I had a bad, indeed very bad time last year. You must know that my life has been turned upside down recently by some painful and tragic events, but now I stubbornly want to get to the bottom of this story, I have to figure out if I'm going crazy". The man is a little embarrassed; he understands that he has a difficult role to play in front of him, "Madam, we can sometimes make mistakes, especially if we are asked without our will. I mean, sometimes when the police question us about a certain murder, maybe it happens that we have no feeling. Therefore, to support the police, we believe or imagine feeling or seeing things, but, precisely because we are enticed by the circumstances, we can make mistakes. When I heard your story, I was at the police station and those words I heard from the investigator entered me, in spite of myself. I had the distinct feeling that it was a real action; it was a story that really happened. I want to explain to you that these feelings I had are genuine, I'm sure because they came to me spontaneously". Sara, "So you confirm to me, for your part, that I really witnessed a murder and the consequent kidnapping of the child?", Ivan, "In my opinion, yes. Of course, and I can't explain why the police didn't find anything and don't believe you!". Sara, gloomy, "They invented the story of Stendhal syndrome; that I had an illness during my visit to the church of Saint Lorenzo. You must know that I am a graduate of letters, specialized in the course of arts and archeology, also interested in architecture. I am sure of what I have seen and experienced. I received the hit to the head, and one of those men gave it to me, I didn't bang my head on the edge of the column base". Ivan, with an understanding attitude, "Madam, I believe you, but I don't know how to give other explanations except that the attack really took place. I repeat and confirm; it really happened. I can't tell you why the police didn't believe you!" Sara does not trust a plausible explanation; the words of the astrologer do not help her much. There is nothing more to say, they say goodbye, but Ivan, before leaving, promises that he will dedicate himself again to this case, and if he has any news, he will call her. Sara at this point is almost forced to give him her phone number, she hesitates, but then agrees, in fact the police are there to assist her in the event of an attempted extortion. She returns to her hotel, and once in the room, she constantly reflects on Ivan's words when he confirmed that the attack really happened; it really happened. She becomes more and more convinced that she really witnessed the attack; yet she immediately afterwards believes that it is almost impossible, "In short, she thinks calmly, the aggression really happened and I was present. Well, I really have the impression of going crazy". Pondering intensely on Ivan's words, she manages to fall asleep. The following day she decides to call the two Christian, who anxiously awaited this call from one day to the next. They decide to meet immediately; Sara finally wants to share the alleged assault she witnessed. Unknowingly she hopes once again for their help. Finally, the three friends meet months after the tragedy; they are sitting on a bench in a city park. Sara has chosen the secluded place; she prefers to avoid telling the story of the aggression in the presence of witnesses, even if involuntary. The two Cristian do everything to show joy to weaken old sadness. They are surprised to see Sara no longer in the grip of her bad memories, but intent on looking for an explanation to recent events, temporarily putting aside her pain. Sara, after demonstrating, or pretending to be relieved, tells the whole story how it happened, or as she saw it in the church of

Saint Lorenzo. She also tells of her hospitalization and the useless police investigations. The two Christians remain to listen to her in silence, but are not surprised by the story of their friend. Sara notices their lack of interest and asks if they were skeptical too! Cris is the first to reply, "Sara, you did nothing but live the story exactly as it happened when the unfortunate Amina and little Sara J were taken away from us! So, you saw a story that you already know, even if it was only told to you". Sara stops for a moment to think, a minute of complete silence fits between them. Then Sara adds, "You're right, but in the story, I think I witnessed, the little girl is stabbed while she tries to escape. It means that little girl had managed to get rid of her tormentor and was running away towards me. Then she was stabbed in the back, which caused her to fall and stop down. At that time her kidnapper immediately reached her, picked her up, and finally they all ran away". Now it is Cristian who responds on impulse, "Sara this is exactly what happened to Sara J, your story fits in everything with what happened to little Sara J, so let's assume that you have somehow relived it, albeit in strangely different circumstances". At the words of her friend, Sara becomes gloomy, she is stiffened, so much so that the two Cristian are frightened and try to comfort and distract her. While they apologize for being so explicit, Sara interrupts them by raising a hand to tell them to shut up, she is always pale and looks at the ground immersed in difficult thoughts, then with a trembling voice, "But I didn't know about Sara J's stabbing. Then,

182

you knew from the first moment that Sara J died this way! Johnalì didn't tell me this detail". The two Cristian are silent; they dare not add anything else. Sara without giving any explanation instantly grabs her cell phone and dials a phone number. Sara's cell phone is calling someone, then when a voice answers, Sara without preamble asks, "Johnalì, I'm in Florence and I'm with Cris and Cristian, they just told me how Sara J was stabbed, but you had not revealed this detail to me! Why! You always knew that Sara J had died this way, but you never revealed it to me!" and she begins to weep for the renewed pain. Johnalì's voice is distinctly heard, replying, "Sara, I didn't tell you at that moment because it was a brutal action beyond any way, and I thought I would hurt you even more by telling you how little Sara J was blocked in an attempt to escape. She looked at me from afar asking for help, and I was shocked by her terrified look. I always knew that she actually died like poor Amina, but I didn't want to put this load on you as well". He interrupts for a moment, they understand that he is also moved, so he continues, "I would have told you one day, I don't know when but I would have told you, probably when the wounds would have started to heal, at least a little. I bet Cristian and Cris told you about it!". Sara answers by explaining to him by phone everything that happened, from the beginning. Meanwhile, the two Cristian talk to each other and try to give an explanation to the alleged vision of Sara. At the end of the long phone call, all three remain silent, each of them meditating on the meaning of these events. Cris breaks the silence trying to understand how Sara saw the scene as it really happened! Neither can give an explanation. Their doubts begin to vanish when Sara decides to talk to them about the contacts she had with the astrologer, listening to this news the two Christian are dismayed, they are both very suggestible. They listen to this story with great curiosity and in the end, both are captured by it, so much so that as soon as Sara finishes her story, they both insist on meeting the astrologer, all together. They should also update him on the latest interesting developments. They absolutely must communicate to the man that Sara did not know how her daughter was stabbed when she was kidnapped. They have lunch at the home of the two Cristian, where they can continue to analyze calmly the story. After lunch they call Ivan, who, happy to be believed and involved again, gives his availability for the next day. In the afternoon, they are still together, and after phoning Johnalì to ask him for his opinion, Sara returns to her hotel room, thanking the two Cristian for their offer to stay at their house. The following day Sara returns to the cemetery, the two Christians are at work and Ivan is available in the afternoon. She sits in front of the family tombstone and leans with her forehead right on Amina's name. She suffers and cries this pain does not give her respite. She always intends to take revenge; in her heart, she never stopped thinking about revenge. She continues to think about the words never said between herself and Amina; to the smiles that will no longer exist between them! She wonders how Sara J would have grown if she had at least reached adolescence, what kind of woman would she become! After crying tears of remorse, she feels a little drained of pain, so she decides to go back to the hotel.

The meeting takes place in a pub, they choose a secluded table, and Sara can hardly overcome Ivan's fears of having found himself, without warning, together with two strangers. All uncertainty vanishes when the two Cristian tell Ivan that they have actively participated in the old events, since they had gone to take back Amina to her Country. During their story, Ivan gradually becomes almost a friend of them. While talking in a very cordial way, they notice that Ivan gets distracted from the conversation several times. Until, while the two talkers continue undaunted in their memories, Ivan interrupts them, "A moment, please. I have a feeling, almost like a reality" and turning his gaze towards nothingness, he adds, "This aggression that Sara witnessed, really happened, it's true, but not now. Now I understand, the aggression did not happen now, but a long time ago...". Everyone is silent, Ivan slowly turning to Sara, adds, "Sara, what era did the clothes of the protagonists of the story belong to? Because this aggression really happened, but in the past, and the dresses could be indicative of that time! ". Sara is baffled, as are the two Christians. Ivan immediately adds, "Maybe this story of the past wants us to understand or reveal something? I don't know, it's like it shows you the solution, or the possibility to really understand what you saw, but only through what happened a long time ago! ". Then he is silent, and everyone else imitates him. After less than a minute, he resumes, "We need to know how that past story happened and we will get information from it for the present. Yes, we need to know how that story went". Cris intervenes, "How? What can we do? Where can we go to find out this story?", and Cristian interrupting everyone by raising his hand, as if he wanted to speak and say something important, "But yes, there are historical archives. The municipal archives in which the relevant events of the various historical periods are reported. We could consult them, even read them one by one, all of them, and find out if this story really happened in the past". Now they are undecided, but Ivan gives the final turning point, "Of course, Cris, good. We have to do just in this way". Sara seems to be able to cling to these last considerations, but then she thinks, for what? What do I need them for; they won't give me back Amina and Sara J. However, she decides to do as suggested. She concentrates and thinks; she goes back with her thoughts to the images of the aggression. She is sure that the woman wore a thick hair gathered on her head by a wide cap, a narrow bust, very narrow, and under the bust a shirt with a wide neckline. She could have seen the wide neckline because during the attack they tore off the shawl the woman was wearing. The woman's skirt was swollen on the hips, as if she had a skirt-holder; however, it was not wide and was short up to above the ankles. The little girl was dressed as a miniature of the woman. Two of the men wore a three-pointed hat and the other two a handkerchief knotted on their heads; all four wore knee-length trousers, and long socks. A couple of them wore only a waistcoat over a wide shirt, while the other two wore a tight knee-length jacket. The clothes were poorly decorated, perhaps only the two men who wore the long jacket, had sleeves with wide lace cuff, same lace cuff even at the end of the trousers. Sara is amazed to be able to remember exactly almost all the clothes; indeed, she was so shocked, that still that story flows before her eyes like a movie. From this first description, quite detailed, those present establish that perhaps the story took place in the seventeenth or eighteenth centuries. Then Sara adds the most poignant memory: the eyes of the little girl, who looked at her terrified while, trying to escape, she was stabbed in the back. Exactly the man who reached her and who allegedly hit her in the head, had the knee-length jacket and the large lace lapels. With this useful information, the next day Sara and Cris will go to ascertain the exact period corresponding to those dresses. They go to a costume historian, one who happens to know Cris. Cris is a costume dressmaker for theatrical performances. The two Christians take a few days off and Ivan too decides to postpone his commitments to devote himself totally to this affair. They finally have the confirmation that the customs are from the late 1700s. Well, now all that remains is to go to the municipal archive and examine the acts of aggression or those recorded at the end of that century. They must first hope that this aggression of the past happened in Florence, and therefore is preserved in the archives of the city. If this were not the case, it would be impossible to trace some evidence of the past. Then, no one is under any illusions, but everyone, each in his heart without confessing it to others, hopes that it is a story that happened in Florence. On the other hand, if this were not the case, Sara would have seen it in another place and not in the church of Saint Lorenzo. In the municipal archive, after asking the clerk for help and advice, there are many volumes to consult. They start with good will, without getting frustrated by the amount of work. A first problem immediately demoralized them: the impossibility of easily understanding the written Italian of that era. They get discouraged, but Sara urges them to say that even if it takes a whole day to decipher a single document, she will spend the rest of her days there deciphering these ancient volumes. Finally, she adds that they are there not by their own will, but because they have been guided by a strange coincidence of events. Sara explains, "If we have been helped by the vision of aggression, we will also be helped in its research". Everyone approves Sara's reasoning and plunges deeply into the delicate volumes. Fortunately, little by little they can understand more and more easily that language written in an ancient way. In the end, they realize that it is just a question of habit to decipher some characters, as well as some words a little different from modern Italian. Meanwhile Johnalì is in almost constant contact with them to keep informed of any developments. He is skeptical, but for the moment, he has understood that this story is useful for Sara, to distract her in some way from her pain.

Unfortunately, the two Cristian end their three days of vacation, Sara and Ivan remain alone in the search. After another day, Ivan is also forced to retire to finish his backlog. Sara, go ahead without being discouraged; another day of research and then another, in the end she too is tired and exhausted. She dejected leaves the archive before five in the afternoon, is really exhausted. Almost to formalize her withdrawal from research, she decides to go for a walking tour out of the house where she lived with Amina. Along the way, she wonders if all of them had fallen victim to an illusion! If that man, Ivan, is a scoundrel! Immersed in these thoughts, she does not notice that she has arrived in front of the house where she lived with Amina, she is about to overcome it without realizing it, when she hears behind her, "e - C - - A A g - C - - ", She jumps, her heart is in her mouth. "It's her, it's Amina!" She whirls around shouting: "AMINAAAAA". There is no one, the street is deserted, but she realizes that she has arrived right in front of her old house. She stops, leans against the wall and aloud, "Amina, my dear. Where are you? Why did you leave me? Excuse me if I did not follow you, if I did not prevent you from going alone, if I neglected you. Excuse me". She cries, and the few passers-by look at her curiously, but no one stops. Sara recovers herself and decides that there is no need to go further with this nonsense of the archive and of the aggression. She doesn't want to waste other people's time too. Without turning around, she greets the house and greets Amina in her heart too, perhaps greets her forever. Yet, at this very moment she is still listening, "e - C - - A A g - C - - ", She has a gasp again, now suddenly she is cheerful, happy, "To hell with all the beliefs and witchcraft. Amina, I understand. I'm sure I'll find the story we're looking for. I'm sure. To hell with my doubts and worries. Tomorrow I will return to the archive. Thank you, Amina,". Sara, happy and invigorated, returns to her hotel; she feels like a lioness ready for any challenge. The following day she is already waiting in front of the closed door of the Municipal Archive. As soon as it opens, she dives into the volumes. Everyone knows her by now, and someone occasionally offers her a coffee or cookies. Sara feels pampered and understood as she continues to leaf through volumes and files. It ends another day of searching, but she does not lose her renewed hope. The next day she always comes back just before opening, her character makes her endure hours of hard reading and boring research. All employees are amazed by her determination. She hasn't told anyone her story, she's careful not to, she knows she'd be considered crazy. This day also ends. The next is Friday; she always returns to the archive early. Today, however, she is encouraged by the help she will receive the following day, when her friends will return to keep her company in the exhausting search. She opens a document and then another. At one point, she finds an anonymous document folded in three, without any writing to identify it. When she opens it, she finds another inside, still folded in three and with a wax seal broken in two. She delicately opens this document and begins to read a story that intrigues her more than the hundreds she has already browsed.

It tells the story of the daughter of a baron, living in the first Florentine hills. The heading of the document refers to the Grand Duchy of Tuscany, at the time of Grand Duke Pietro Leopoldo of Lorraine, 1781. "Well, Sara thinks, at least we are in the right period". Continuing to read, she gradually became passionate about the story of Baroness Giuliana, betrothed since birth to a Florentine viscount. Her father had promised her to a man twenty years older than her, in order to be related to a more important and more powerful family. The document also contains comments by the judge, one of which refers to the need to clarify the previous events of the family, in order to reach a verdict.

At the age of fourteen, Baroness Giuliana was married to the Viscount. The unfortunate woman had refused to marry him, and throughout the ceremony, she always cried. Then there is a note, "The first complaint came to this court of the Grand Duchy when the new wife of the Viscount, Baroness Giuliana, seems to have disappeared after a month from the marriage". The two families appealed to the court on mutual charges. From some investigations, it has been verified that Baroness Giuliana escaped to the Republic of Lucca with such a young Mr. Flavio, her secret lover. Unfortunately, this court cannot intervene on the family of the young "kidnapper" Mr. Flavio as a citizen of Lucca resident in another jurisdiction, (Lucca being a city-state independent of the Grand Duchy). Here ends this brief annotation of the cause for kidnapping.

Then Sara finds another file, this time still sealed. She doesn't know what to do, she looks around and decides to detach the wax seal from the sheet, avoiding breaking it. She wants to find the underlying of this story. The new document always refers to the court of the Grand Duchy and bears the date of 1787. Continuing to read, she discovers that a murdered woman has been found just outside the church of Saint Lorenzo in Florence. They found her with two dagger slashes in her chest. After some investigations, this Court has verified that it is the body of Baroness Giuliana, who fled six years earlier with her young lover Mr. Flavio and since that time resident in Lucca. Then the Court summons the brother of the baroness, being her father died a few months earlier, also summons the viscount her ex-husband, who in the meantime has proceeded to remarry after having repudiated in absentia the young wife fugitive. From the first interrogations, both the woman's brother and her ex-husband declare themselves unrelated to the crime. This Court, despite the difficulties due to the total lack of witnesses, continues the investigation and unexpectedly receives a decisive revelation from the family of the baroness's young lover of Lucca, Mr. Flavio.

Strangely, the official documents end here, the writing turns into a chronicle written by some employee of the court, a chronicle that is told and no longer official, that is, no longer officially released by the Court. Sara read on. After a few days, two well-known hitmen are arrested, linked to the family of the former groom, the viscount. Yet the court with great regret fails to get any confession from the two hitmen. Then Sara reads a footnote: *"With great regret, the two hitmen cannot be interrogated with torture after it has just been abolished, in 1786 by this Grand Duchy, as a means of making criminals confess"*. The scribe resumes writing. It seems that the two killers confessed not to the court, but to the Baroness's family, *"with unreliable methods"*, that they had been hired to kidnap the woman in the church of Saint Lorenzo in Florence. For this reason, they are brought before this court by the baron, brother of Baroness Giuliana. The court does not consider the poor physical conditions in which the two hitmen are, which show evident signs of violence and torture, but accepts their confession made in a "spontaneous" way.

Sara realizes that Giuliana's brother tortured them and convinced them to talk. The two hitmen reveal the names of two other accomplices, who are immediately captured and interrogated. With the wit of the court, in the end, history is reconstructed. On the death of the father of the Baroness Giuliana, Mr. *"Unknown"*, as the Court calls him, (it is known that he is Giuliana's ex-husband Viscount, but he is not named because there are no clear charges against him), hires the four henchmen to kidnap ex-wife Giuliana. Meanwhile, he summons Giuliana with deception in the church of Saint Lorenzo. The four hitmen were hidden, they saw not a single woman come as agreed, but accompanied by a girl more or less the age of six. This detail upset the kidnapping plan, indeed, having to hurry to avoid being discovered, three of them jumped on the woman and the fourth grabbed the child. In the fight, both women screamed, attracting people's attention, so, to silence them, the woman was stabbed in the chest, but the girl, freed from her grip, was running away. The only way to stop her was to hit her with a knife in the back, then the little girl fell to the ground injured. The four henchmen picked them up both and immediately fled. However, by now it was late, the people had gathered, so as soon as the killers realized that the woman was dead, they abandoned her just outside the church. They took the little girl with them as she was still breathing. Interviewed by the Court, they replied that they had to deliver the woman to two men at the Sienese mill in the Florentine countryside. When they reached the mill, they only managed to deliver the child in serious bad condition. They have not been able to give answers on the identity of those to whom they have delivered the child. They repeated that they did not know the two men to whom they delivered the injured child to the mill and where they then took her. They could only see that the two men were in an elegant carriage and that the child had been placed in the seat.

Sara is shocked. She knows this is the scene she saw. She is sure of it. She is excited, now she begins to guess the fate of the child. The story of the court case ends here. Sara closes the file, but as she folds it, she sees a reference to another file, a code made up of letters and numbers, which allows her to track down a last file. She opens it quickly, but this time there is no court heading, even if it is part of the chronicles of the time. Sara discovers that it is a letter to the court of the Grand Duchy and coming from Lucca. It tells the story following the death of the woman and the kidnapping of her daughter. It is the family of a rich Lucca merchant, a certain Mr. Flavio, and mentions without naming him, a Florentine baron, whose sister had been killed in mysterious circumstances. This man of Lucca, Mr. Flavio, had secretly informed the Florentine baron that his sister Giuliana, when she had fled to Lucca seven years earlier, was already pregnant with her legitimate husband. She later gave birth to the baby girl in Lucca, where the girl grew up, considering Mr. Flavio as her father. When they found the body of the dead woman outside the church of Saint Lorenzo, no trace of the child was found. Mr. Flavio made some investigations even though he could not go in person to the Grand Duchy of Tuscany. From his investigations, it emerged that the girl should now presumably be in the viscount's house in Florence. The document says nothing else. It concludes by specifying that both the baron, Giuliana's brother, and this gentleman from Lucca, had insisted on having news of the little girl. Finally, only after much insistence, the viscount declared privately, without leaving any documents, through his trusted man, that the child is his bastard daughter and that she is being kept in their palace. He adds that it is not the viscount's intention to report further information. The viscount wants to protect the child, he repeats, his bastard daughter, and protect the name of his House. He recommends that everyone desist from any further investigation or request. The document concludes the story by also reporting a declaration from the man from Lucca, Mr. Flavio, who declares that the child is the legitimate daughter of the viscount, since Baroness Giuliana was already pregnant when she arrived in Lucca. However, the viscount, while knowing that his wife was pregnant when she ran away, insists that the child is the result of his relationship with a servant, to avoid a serious scandal.

Sara would like to read more news, but in spite of herself, there are no further documents. Now everything is clear to her. The little girl, as declared by the viscount, is alive, a prisoner in the house of her legitimate father, but raised as a bastard daughter. The viscount does not want to spread the news that his ex-wife, the Baroness Giuliana, when she betrayed him by taking refuge in Lucca, was already pregnant with his heir. He has taken the child back, but for everyone she is his bastard and not his natural daughter. Sara has a strange premonition; it seems clear to her that this story of the past is similar to that of Amina and Sara J.

Yes, she is sure; Sara J is alive. She screams with joy, "Yes, Sara J is alive." Those present turn to her, but she does not pay attention to them. She quickly clicks with her mobile phone the pages she has just read and goes out to give the good news to Ivan and hear his opinion. Ivan, as soon as he hears the whole story, asks her to meet him immediately. Shortly after, sitting in a park, Ivan reads what was written badly, as the photos with the mobile phone were taken quickly, but he listens to Sara's story. He too is convinced that Sara J is alive. The two rejoice, finally both Ivan and Sara have an explanation for their strange visions and perceptions. They call the two Christians telling them what had happened in a confused way, and the two insist on staying where they are, as they would have immediately joined them. Then, Sara, without wasting time, immediately calls Johnalì too. As soon as the two Christians reach them, they find Sara still on the phone with Johnalì; there is a new valid hope. Sara would like to go to the police to explain everything, but Ivan stops her and warns her that she doesn't really have proof yet. Sara insists, she will make the police understand and accept this story. Because of her insistence, not only Ivan, but also the two Christian try to make her desist, even Johnalì, on her phone, asks her not to do anything, to return immediately to London and sleep on it. Everyone advises her to stay calm and not come to hasty conclusions, but Sara does not listen to anyone, she wants her little Sara J back. They all decide to go to dinner at the home of the two Christian. During dinner, they do nothing but re-examine this story described in the archive. Perhaps the two Christian are still skeptical, but they don't want to blame Sarah; they think she is still too weak for the loss of her family. Ivan is the only one to encourage her and give her hope, and the two Christian get angry with him because of Ivan's condescending attitude towards Sara. Between considerations and assumptions, the evening arrives early; everyone retires to the homes. Sara returns to the hotel, and alone in her room, she develops the idea of having to go to Amina's Country to look for Sara J. The little one is alive; she is more than sure. She is very happy, even if she is always afraid that all this is just an illusion, but for this very reason, to dispel any doubts, she unquestionably decides to go to Amina's Country to track down Sara J. The following day she meets Ivan and the two Christians again, the first argues that it is right to go and look for Sara J, while the other two, terrified, reiterate that it would be a mistake to go there. Anyway, Sara has decided. The following day she takes the plane to return to London and immediately organize the trip to the other coast of the Mediterranean. It doesn't matter if she forgot to start the paperwork for the transfer of Amina's urn from Florence to London, then she'll take care of it.

The Hope.

As soon as she arrives in London, she wastes no time, immediately starts planning the trip. Johnalì goes to meet her with the hope of dissuading her. He explains that she is about to commit suicide. He saw the little girl stabbed. Even if she had survived, she would surely have bled to death, certainly not being able to be assisted by a doctor. Sara is determined, she firmly believes that Sara J is alive somewhere, and that with the help of Amina's cousin, Ali, or Anbar, and why not with the help of mother Raissa, she will be able to find her little girl. She must do it for Sara J, for Amina, for herself and for justice. She confesses to Johnalì that she intends to kill the kidnapper, who will surely be that wretched ex-husband of Amina, and adds bursting into tears, that she is sure that Adel is an accomplice. Johnalì, holds her in his arms and tries to console her, realizes that Sara is still suffering. He begins to believe that Sara will never recover, at least until she has tried everything she can. He remains silent for a while with Sara in his arms, then he says to her, "Sara, Sara, listen to me, if you really think you want to commit suicide in this crazy adventure, I will not leave you alone. I will try to help you in all ways". Sara looks at him surprised and confident, waiting for her friend to add more. Johnalì continues, "You know that I come from the same land as Amina, I know those places well. Before coming to Great

Britain, I was leading a life on the verge of legality, indeed I was a criminal. This is why I decided to leave my country and immigrate to Europe at the age of twenty, to avoid ending my life in jail or worse, killed by police officers or a rival gang. I should have gone to France, as is more natural for a people like mine who speak French as a second language, but in France, my friends would have easily found me. I wanted to give a total cut to my past, only about five years after my move to London; my parents joined me. For reasons of balance between my previous life and the current one, I have not abandoned my old contacts, but I have no longer participated in their activity. They didn't bother me or force me to collaborate with them, on the contrary we are still friends and we respect each other", he stops and Sara hugs him, and then adds: "Basically they are indebted to me, in a certain way, and it seems that now is the time to ask for their help". Sara is radiant with happiness, she does not yet know how her friend will help her, but Johnalì word is enough. However, Johnalì tries to dampen her optimism by warning her that it will be very difficult and risky, and that she will have to stay out of it because he will have to interact with important and dangerous people. Will Sara always be able to stay out of it? Sara makes him understand that she would face an arena of lions and that she has already managed to do it on her own when she went to take back the unfortunate Amina. Johnalì does not want to hear reasons, but finally he is forced to surrender at the absolute insistence of the woman. Indeed, reflects Johnalì, Sara's very discreet presence could be useful for identifying people and places. Well, Sara is infinitely grateful to Johnalì, who goes away adds jokingly "I do it for my partner, Sara J is always Amina's daughter and therefore heir to her part of the pub". Following the good news of this unexpected help, Sara is more serene, she also resumes her work after months of interruption. A few days pass and Johnalì does not mention the journey in search of Sara J. For her part, Sara does not want to rush him, from what she has been able to understand, this time people are far more dangerous than those two scarecrows of Adel and the ex-Amina's husband. However, this lack of communication casts her doubts on Johnalì's will or ability to help her. Until finally Johnalì, one evening, while they are at the pub, calls her aside at the back, Andrea also takes part in the conversation. Johnalì confides to her that he has made contact with his former "friends", and that they are happy to see him again and help him. Then he explains, "Please, what I tell you is very important, no one should know about your relationship, I mean about the marriage between you and Amina. Everyone in Amina's country must know that Amina had taken refuge in your house and that you welcomed her and helped her to rebuild her life". Johnalì adds that he will go first, to Amina's country, with all the details of the various addresses and photos of the people involved. Once he meets his former friends, they will first check if Sara J is alive or dead. After that, in case she is alive, they will organize her escape. Sara gives him Amina's parent phone and Alif's phone.

By chance, she in addition, has a photo of Adel, and has the old address of Amina's husband, where they went to get her to escape to Italy. Unfortunately, she has nothing else, but Johnalì reassures her that it might be enough for a start; his friends will try to retrieve the other addresses and possibly take updated photos of all the people involved. Johnalì then summarizes in more detail: in a first phase, his friends will try to find out where Adel and Amina's ex-husband live, both are hiding with false personal data to escape Amina's complaint years ago. After that, only he will go and check, along with his friends, if Sara J is still alive. In case they find her alive, Sara will join them to help pick up Sara J. Probably the little girl will only trust Sara, maybe not even Johnalì! In any case, for this last phase it will be better if Sara will be present on site. Once the child is freed, Sara will take her to Europe with a deep-sea speedboat, but this time they will have a smuggler almost dedicated only to the two of them, as it will be a speedboat for the transport of contraband goods. Sara is enthusiastic, finally someone will take care of her; all the life she has always fought alone for her rights and her dear ones, now she feels pampered, and is happy about it, even if her character is quite independent, as an alpha female. Having passed the information to his friends, Johnalì just has to wait and hope. Couples of weeks are gone and still no news. Sara is silent and continues her work as if these were normal days for her, she does not want to hurry, and she has complete confidence in her friend. Finally, the first news arrives, and Johnalì immediately contacts Sara; now it's the end of March. Still this news is not entirely satisfactory, if on the one hand it was quite easy to find Adel's new address, unfortunately they cannot find that of Amina's ex-husband. The problem is that they don't have a picture of him. They would have to kidnap Adel and convince him to reveal the new identity and new address of Amina's ex-husband, but this would raise a fuss and attract the attention of the police, while instead they would have to act in absolute silence. Then Johnalì explains to Sara that it would be best to contact Anbar directly; she is sure to have a wedding photo of her sister Amina, or a photo of her ex-brother-in-law. Approaching Anbar shouldn't be difficult, they discover that Anbar has returned to her parents' home since she found out she was used and deceived by her husband for the trip to France. She preferred to leave despite suffering from the separation from her children, who, for the parental authority, remained at her husband's house. They also managed to learn that Amina's father died of a heart attack about a month ago; his heart could not resist the latest events. He loved Amina very much even though he did not know how to defend her. "Well, Sara replies, it means I will speak incognito with Anbar. She will certainly collaborate with me, if only to avenge her sister's death and maybe she can give us more information about Sara J". Johnalì is hesitant, he would not want to expose his friend so early in this operation, however it seems that there is no other solution. Both decide to leave within a week, just the right time for the necessary documents. They will travel together, and will stay in the same hotel, although they will take another room in another hotel as a safety haven in case it will be necessary to escape the first hotel. The two Christians are informed of the trip and its purpose. They keep all the telephone numbers that Sara and Johnalì will use, with the peremptory order to only receive phone calls and absolutely never call one of these numbers on their own initiative.

On the day of departure, Sara thinks that eleven months have now passed since Amina's murder and Sara J's alleged kidnapping. Now Sara J, if she had been alive, would have turned seven. Sara is afflicted and tormented to know that for all these months Sara J has been left alone, without her family. Alone with her mother's killers. They may also have led Sara J to believe her friends in Italy abandoned her. Surely, they will have plagiarized and indoctrinated her with lies. Sara hopes that a year is not so much for a little girl, maybe Sara J is still waiting for someone to come and save her! She spent the trip absorbed in these thoughts. Finally, they arrive at their destination. As soon as the plane lands, they go to the first hotel, where they leave their suitcases and then immediately to the second hotel, where they leave other suitcases. They decide to rest one in a hotel and the other in the other, and both order a dinner in the room for two. The next day, Johnalì comes to Sara and brings her some local clothes, then both, driving a car loaned by a friend of Johnalì's, approach the house of Amina's parents. According to the information obtained, Anbar lives alone with her mother and a cousin, the son of her father's brother. Her brother Adel's also visits them occasionally and provides for their needs, but despite this, sometimes Anbar and her cousin go out for normal daily chores. Sara and Johnalì are in the car, not far from the house. Luckily, for them, already on the first day of waiting they see them go out, they are Anbar and a boy, certainly the cousin. They leave the car and follow them on foot from a certain distance. While Anbar with his cousin goes around the vegetable stalls, Sara and Johnalì get closer and closer until the moment when another accomplice, a friend of Johnalì, intervenes, pretending to argue with Johnalì. As a diversion, the two pretend to come to blows and in the fight, they fall on Anbar's cousin. At that precise moment, Sara approaches Anbar and puts a note in her hand. Anbar is amazed; a stranger gives her a note? She does not know what to think and remains with the note in her hand without hiding it. To make her understand what happens, Sara slightly lifts her veil and reveals herself to the woman. Anbar spreads her arms to hug her, but Sara can't risk being discovered or above all wasting time, so the only solution to stop the woman is to punch her in the stomach. While Anbar gasps in pain, Sara whispers in her ear, "Sorry but we're in camouflage, read the note I gave you. Bye, see you soon". Meanwhile, Johnalì and his accomplice, after making sure that the message was passed to Anbar, disappear immediately, before a police officer intervenes. Anbar's cousin protests and yells at the two men, then putting himself in order, still shaken, reaches his cousin. Anbar recovers from the fist and hides the ticket very well; then they continue shopping at the market. Sara and Johnalì are happy; the first action went well. In the note they wrote that, they came to look for Anima's ex-husband and that she must help them by delivering a photo of him. They add that the next day or the day after, Sara and an accomplice would return to the house and follow her to the market, where the photo will be delivered. The next day, a friend of Johnalì's goes to wait for Anbar outside the house, better not to risk, perhaps Anbar has been discovered or perhaps she has no intention of cooperating. Sara and another accomplice friend wait a short distance away, waiting for a phone call to notify them when Anbar and her cousin are leaving. Johnalì does not show up, the Anbar cousin could recognize him for the fight the day before, and guess something. That day no one leaves Amina's parent house. It may be normal not to have to go out the next day, or they may have discovered the trick! Sara does not lose heart and Johnalì too. After another day, the same stakeout, when they finally see the two leave the house. They enter the market followed by Johnalì's friend, and further away by Sara with a second accomplice. Anbar looks around several times to try to see her friend, but Sara out of caution remains hidden, they are afraid of a trap. After a while, Sara gathers courage and approaches Anbar, unaware that her chaperone has a silenced pistol, ready to shoot Anbar and her cousin in case they set up an ambush against Sara. Fortunately, Anbar manages to pass an envelope to Sara, who instantly hides it under her dress, then immediately walks away. Then Sara and her accomplice first take a long walk to avoid being followed, and then go back to the hotel where Johnalì, also recently arrived, is waiting for her. They open the envelope and find two photos of Anima's ex-husband, plus a letter from Anbar explaining, *"I was deceived by my husband. He had set a trap for me to bring out the unfortunate Amina. They had led me to believe that we were going to Marseille for a business visit to my brother, and I had unknowingly informed Amina that we would meet. After writing to her to go to Marseille on time, which is the day before the trip; my husband unexpectedly took me to his cousin's house in the countryside, along with my two children. I was confined, without a cell phone at my disposal. At that moment, I could no longer communicate with Amina, and I no longer knew anything. I was desperate, I felt that something had happened, but I never imagined they would kill Anima. So, all the deception became clear. In desperation, I ran away to take refuge at my parents' house. I took my two children with me, but my husband was able to take them back not only by having parental authority over them, but also because I ran away by abandoning him. I'm sure my husband is also responsible for Amina's death and I didn't want to live with an accomplice in my sister's murder. I hope you can find my sister's killer and punish him, as he deserves. I haven't seen my husband since he came to pick up my two children"*. In the letter she makes no reference to Sara J, perhaps Anbar has not been informed of anything about the fate of the child! The photos are immediately passed to those in charge of tracing the last piece of the mosaic. Another three days of feverish waiting pass, and then finally they receive other indications: the house where Amina's ex-husband resides has been found. It changed its name and is now called Afiq. "Afiq! Johnalì says, other than honest, that scoundrel". In the meantime, they have ascertained that no girl of Sara J's age lives in Adel's house. The last hope, if Sara J were alive, would be to find her at Afiq's house. Indeed, the man is her legitimate father. Now they cannot act, at least until they are certain that Sara J is really living with Afiq. They discovered that the man lives with a new wife and that he has three children: the first of four years, the second of three and the third of two, and his wife is pregnant with the fourth. He lives in a suburb of the city, almost on the edge of the desert, in a place where he has no relatives as neighbors. In addition to his family, they found that two other people live in their home, but have not yet identified who they are. Sara would like to go directly to Afiq and violently break into the house, but she knows this is not possible. They have to wait and wait; in the meantime, they change both hotels and, to look like tourists, join a group for a sightseeing tour in the south of the Country. One late afternoon, while Sara and Johnalì, pretending to be tourists, sip their tea seated at an elegant table by the sea, Johnalì's phone rings. The man replies and, after a short communication, asks Sara to go back to the hotel with him. Sara is surprised; she wants to know who called. Johnalì replies that he will tell her everything in the room. Sara is tense, she fears it could be bad news, otherwise why didn't he answer right away? She is going to faint, but she knows she doesn't have to attract attention, she braces up and they go to their room. Just inside, she takes a deep breath and looks at Johnalì anxiously. The man takes her in his arms and gives her the good news, the news they hoped to receive: Sara J is alive. Both rejoice, embrace happily and Sara screams and cries for happiness. Johnalì calms her down and reminds her to be silent, then adds that Sara J is imprisoned at Afiq's house with his family and Afiq's unmarried sister. Sara asks him why he did not immediately communicate this good news leaving her in doubt, but Johnalì justifies himself by explaining that he feared a reaction of uncontrolled joy, a reaction that would have drawn attention to them. Sara lets herself fall on the bed and remains with her gaze fixed on the ceiling; she goes back with her mind to the good times. She does not care how they manage to free her, or how they will return to Italy, for her great fortune, Johnalì has powerful friends; although he insists that they are very dangerous friendships. Now they have to implement the last part of the plan. Meanwhile, they update the two Cristian using previously agreed code words. At the news of the discovery of the little girl alive, also the two Cristian scream with joy. They know that now it's their turn to take action. They must go near the south coast, to a strategic central point, ready to intervene and reach the two refugee women.

Surely, it will be the shore of some beach in the Sicilian Mediterranean. As soon as possible, they will also receive the name of the place, but in the meantime, they leave.

In the morning scheduled for action, they know that all the women are in the house, while Afiq is at work. They decided to intervene when the family is reunited: better to hold it all hostage. A local woman, an accomplice, goes to the door of Afiq's house with a beautiful bouquet of flowers, Sara is also with her, but she is well covered so as not to be recognized as European. She rings the bell, someone from the apartment asks who it is, and the woman replies that she has a bouquet of flowers for the landlady from her husband. Afiq's younger sister opens the door; she is a 15-year-old girl. As soon as she opens, the woman passes the flowers in the girl's arms telling her that they are on her brother's side. The girl is forced to take them, keeping her hands busy holding the flowers. At this precise moment the woman instantly puts a cloth soaked in chloroform tightly on her face, and lays the sleeping girl on the ground. Then a voice from the other room, asks the girl who has rung the doorbell? The accomplice replies that she is delivering a bouquet of flowers by the landlord. At this precise moment, they both enter the room where they find everyone sitting in front of the television. Sara enters first so that she is immediately seen by Sara J and does not alarm her. As soon as she sees Sara J among the other children, she discovers her face and calls her. Sara J is stunned, but it doesn't take long for her to run and jump into Sara's arms, clutching her tightly. The little girl does not cry or despair; she clings tightly to her adoptive mother and does not want to give up for any reason. The accomplice first runs towards Afiq's wife, immediately silencing her with another handkerchief soaked in chloroform, then, while Sara walks into the corridor with Sara J, three other accomplices enter the apartment and go instantly to the room where the whole family is gathered. The three men help their accomplice to anesthetize quickly the children as well. No one in the house has had time to realize what is happening: from the entrance of the two women with the bouquet of flowers, to the narcotization of everyone present, only a little more than a minute has passed. Before putting them to sleep, the woman reassured the children by whispering in a low voice not to worry, that their mother is sleeping and that they would now be asleep too. With the whole family asleep and tied up in the bedroom, Sara, holding Sara J in her arms, sneaks out of the apartment. As soon as she goes into the street she walks slowly towards the corner of the building, with difficulty she goes around the corner, still with Sara J in her arms, she gets into the car where, in addition to the driver, there is Johnali. Sara J as soon as she sees him, hugs him happy and peaceful. Then the car starts. The four accomplices remain in the apartment, patiently awaiting Afiq's return, making sure that the family continues to sleep. In the meantime, they left a letter prominently on the table in the dining room. In the letter it is written, *"Don't dare look for little Sara J. If you try to look for her, we come back to kill you and your wife. Your family is fine, it is only narcotized and they will wake up only late in the evening, if they have any problem, make them drink some vials that we left you on the table. Don't even try to call a doctor or the police".* Meanwhile the car with Sara J continues its long journey towards the coast. They are headed to a building near a boarding site. Sara already has experience with smugglers, yet Johnalì reassures her by explaining that the smuggler is a safe person and that she will travel with another couple as well as several crates of smuggling goods. The crossing will be carried out with an offshore motorboat equipped with two powerful engines. She doesn't have to worry, because until she leaves, he'll be there with them. At a certain moment, in the open desert, they leave the car with the driver and move on to a tarpaulin van loaded with goats. They settle at the bottom of the van, in a small compartment where they take their place together with the bad smell of goats. Finally, more than four hours have passed since they left Afiq's house, when Johnalì receives a phone call, he speaks briefly and after hanging up he explains in a low voice to Sara, so as not to be understood by Sara J, that everything went well. As soon as Afiq entered the house, they beat him to scare him and then stunned him with a strong blow to the head. Finally, they placed him on the ground with the letter clearly visible next to him. Before leaving, they wanted to leave a perennial sign of his infamy: they scarred his face by wounding him on the cheek with the knife. Surely as soon as he recovers, if he can move right away, he will read the letter and find the still sleeping bodies of his family. They are all sure that he will not notify the police; rather he will take care of his injuries and his family primarily. If he's smart, he'll think it's best to leave the girl. However, Johnalì's friends, in about a month, the time that Afiq heals from the wounds received, will communicate to the police the domicile and the new identity of the man, to ensure him to justice. Once in Italy they will decide how to justify Sara J's escape to report the kidnappers. Sara is serene and satisfied; everything went well. She already knows that she will arrange with Anbar to reconstruct Sara J's escape to pursue the case against her kidnappers and Amina's killers. Absorbed in these thoughts, they arrive by the sea, near a house with a large vegetable garden all around. They stealthily descend and head to a hut behind the main building. It seems that there is no one. They stay there a few minutes until a man arrives and talks to Johnalì briefly, leaving him bundles, 2 life jackets and several bottles of water to drink. Johnalì returns to them and delivers all the stuff along with some food and chocolate that he has previously prepared. Now they have to rest, as they will leave late at night. Sara takes advantage of the hours of waiting to explain the whole story to Sara J. She discovers that Sara J knew of her mother's death, indeed her father had threatened her telling her that if she ran away, she would meet the same fate as her mother. The little girl was terrified and she was waiting for someone to come and free her, but she had little hope. She was convinced that everyone had died, even Sara, at least so her father had said. The little girl says that luckily, she could understand the orders they gave her, since Amina often spoke with her using her mother tongue, and this was useful to her. Then she explains that Afiq's wife, when she gave her orders, did not admit that she wasted time. In the house, she did the cleaning and all the most demanding work. Yet, her three stepsiblings were not mean to her. Johnalì as soon as he knows the destination in Italy calls the two Cristian, who were terribly in pain, not receiving news. He reassures them by mentioning that everything is fine and then tells them the location of landing. They must be there the next day very early in the morning. The two Cristian would like to talk to Sara J and Sara, but it is not prudent. After the phone call, Johnalì destroys the cell phone by burning it. Two young boys join the two women; they are two brothers, in addition to the heavy load. Finally, it is evening, everyone is worried about the conditions of the sea, it is agitated and they expect a worsening. Johnalì wants them to postpone the journey, but Sara has confidence in the powerful motorboat, having already made the same crossing on a much less safe dinghy. She tries to convince her friend to let her leave, and Johnalì gives in only when the smuggler tells him that, if they skip this trip, for his part the next one will be only after four days. The alternatives are either to leave now with this motorboat, or to wait four days, or, finally, to look for another passage. Johnalì and Sara consider it too risky to wait four days, they don't know Afiq's reaction once awake, and so they decide to leave. At the agreed signal, everyone leaves the hut and heads for the motorboat. As always, they walk at least three kilometers before reaching the boarding point on the seashore. Arriving at the motorboat, they realize that it is a fishing motorboat with an open cruiser, and two large engines. Johnalì would like to make Sara back off, but she insists on leaving. Some men are still loading it with many crates, and, as soon as all the goods are loaded, they embark the four passengers. Before going up the two women hug Johnalì strongly, Sara tries to reassure him, tells him not to worry, they will meet again next time directly in London. She has only one request, she beg Johnalì, to ask the smuggler to place her and Sara J in the bow. The smuggler accepts, and at the end, they say goodbye as the motorboat turns on the engines and leaves. From their looks of understanding, they both understand that this trip will be risky due to the sea conditions. Sara pretends not to notice the danger or even her fear. As agreed, no one will have to call Johnalì before three days. Thus, as soon as they arrive at their destination, they will meet the two Cristian and will not communicate immediately with Johnalì in the event that someone spies him on. The speedboat quickly moves away from the shore. As the hull moves away Sara sees Johnalì disappear a little at a time, until darkness envelops everything. Sara thoughtfully ties Sara J to her with a strap, then both hold tight to the strings of the crates tied to the bow. As soon as they enter the Middle Mediterranean, the sea ripples and agitates becoming dangerous, so much, so that the helmsman is forced to reduce the speed. They are tossed in the dark at the mercy of the rough sea, and terror takes possession of them. With each jump of the motorboat, everyone jumps, landing badly and painfully on the crates. It seems to be getting worse and worse, the helmsman forces the two boys to drain the water they embark with buckets, the two reluctantly accept, and to obey the helmsman, they are forced to give up the ropes to which they are firmly clinging. The two engines are striving more and more, and the speed is further reduced, while remaining sustained. The two Sara are terrified and hold each other tighter and tighter, tied together and clinging to the ropes of the crates, wet by the waves that become higher and higher. As they try to unload the water on board, a wave stronger than the others blows up the motorboat, causing it to land almost on its side and take water until it cannot continue the journey. The helmsman decides to turn off the engines and shouts that everyone must empty the water on board. Unfortunately, only now do they realize that one of the two boys disappeared, fell into the sea. The other is desperate, calling him screaming and trying to locate him among the high waves in the dark. Unfortunately, no one answers, the boy seems to have been swallowed by the sea. They can't find it even using a powerful flashlight, stop in the middle of the waves risk everyone going to the bottom. The surviving boy, instead of working to empty the motorboat as the helmsman and Sara do, desperately continues to call his brother. Seeing no one and receiving no answer, he also dives into the water, disappearing into the waves. Sara is terrified, the helmsman didn't have time to stop him; he scans the waves as far as possible in an attempt to locate at least the second boy. After a few minutes another wave threatens to overturn the motorboat, the helmsman himself is about to fall into the water, but manages to keep himself on the stern railing, then turns on the engines and they leave quickly. Sara is petrified, it could also have happened to her and the little girl to fall into the water, fortunately, she has secured her place in the bow and she too remains firmly clinging to the ropes of the crates. However, the disappearance in the waves of those two unfortunate boys leave her terrified and worried about her fate and Sara J'. Thus continues the journey towards the coast among the increasingly threatening waves. Sara looks towards the coast and prays, prays that they will arrive safely on the shore. She observes little Sara J, who in the meantime has always remained crouched against her with her eyes tightly closed in fear. Perhaps the little girl did not even notice that the two boys disappeared into the waves. The motorboat heads tenaciously towards the still distant shore, and Sara too remains tenaciously clinging to the motorboat with the little one tied to her.